Her Write

HIS NAME

THOEMMES

PLATONICS
A STUDY

Ethel M. Arnold

With a new Introduction by
Phyllis Wachter

THOEMMES PRESS

© Thoemmes Press 1995

Published in 1995 by
Thoemmes Press
11 Great George Street
Bristol BS1 5RR
England

ISBN 1 85506 389 1

This is a reprint of the 1894 Edition
© Introduction by Phyllis Wachter 1995

Publisher's Note

INTRODUCTION

I remember being asked after returning from a pilgrimage to Wales whether the 'Ladies of Llangollen', two women who shared a romantic friendship during the late eighteenth and early nineteenth-centuries, were lesbian.[1] I had to admit that even after viewing a portrait of the pair in their riding habits and beaver hats and gazing at the bed in which they slept together for over fifty years, I was in no better position to answer the question than before the outset of my journey. Actually, I felt that the nature of these women's sexuality mattered little because what was most significant about their composite life-stories was that they made the trek from Ireland to Wales to seek financial independence, emotional sustenance, and intellectual stimulation in relationship with each other.

Unlike these ladies, Ethel M. Arnold was never identified with any one romantic friendship, yet her writings, especially her novel, *Platonics: A Study* (1894), reveal that Arnold's muse was the idealization of an abstract female beloved.[2] I was, therefore, not surprised when one of Arnold's surviving relatives asked me over tea, 'Do you think Ethel was a lesbian?' My answer was just as tentative as it had been with the 'Ladies of Llangollen'; I automatically directed the

---

[1] Elizabeth Mavor, Introduction, *The Ladies of Llangollen: A Study in Romantic Friendship* (Middlesex, England: Penguin Books, 1971).

[2] Ethel M. Arnold, *Platonics: A Study* (London: Osgood, McIlvaine and co., 1894).

question back to my questioner who then conveniently opted to change the subject. Considering how difficult it can be to establish the range and diversity of a person's intimate relationships when given today's atmosphere of relative candour, it would be pointless to impose labels like 'lesbian' or 'gay' on people who lived during eras when such words either did not exist or were not used to describe the very individuals for whom they were intended. What can be said is that during the nineteenth century, there were women like Ethel Arnold who were not necessarily self-defined lesbians but whose lives and texts were informed by other women. Even if Arnold and some of her close female friends were, in fact, 'lesbian', in the carnal sense of the word, such a label limits our appreciation of the full range of feelings, attitudes, and behaviours which constitute same-sex relationships between women.

According to Gordon Haight, 'the Victorians' conception of love between those of the same sex cannot be fairly understood by an age steeped in Freud', since 'the modern reader suspects perversion' where the Victorians 'saw only beautiful friendship' (p. xv).[3] Most people were completely ignorant of 'female inversion or perversion' including Queen Victoria herself who refused to sign the 1885 Labouchère Amendment which 'sought to penalize private homosexual acts by two years' imprisonment' until 'all reference to such practices' by women was omitted (p. 418).[4] Besides, since all respectable Victorian women were considered

---

[3] Gordon S. Haight, Introduction, *Edith Simcox and George Eliot*, by K. A. McKenzie (Oxford: Oxford University Press, 1961).

[4] Blanche Wiesen Cook, 'Female Support Networks and Political Activism', *A Heritage of her Own*, editors Nancy F. Cott and Elizabeth H. Pleck (New York: Simon and Schuster, 1979), pp. 412–44.

'passionless',[5] it was assumed that women could not 'respond with enthusiasm to the advances of men' let alone 'stimulate sexual excitement between themselves' (p. 118).[6] As a result of this masking of sexual expression by Victorian women, there is little way of knowing the extent to which women acted out or even verbalized feelings of passionate attraction toward each other.[7] Yet, although lesbianism may not have been 'a category for organizing and defining women's emotional and sexual experience' in the Victorian world (p. 584),[8] an increased preoccupation with the concept of male homosexuality in legal and literary circles eventually suggested the existence of a female version of 'the love that dare not speak its name'.[9] It is apparent that whereas same-sex bonding was considered perfectly natural during the eighteenth and most of the nineteenth centuries to the extent that it was encouraged as an integral part of a young girl's upbringing, gradually public opinion became less tolerant of close adult female friendships, especially when they influenced women to consider career and lifestyle alternatives to home, family, and marriage. As a result, today, it is necessary to develop a new vocabulary for addressing

---

[5] Nancy F. Cott, 'Passionlessness: An Interpretation of Victorian Sexual Ideology, 1790–1850', *A Heritage of her Own*, editors Nancy F. Cott and Elizabeth H. Pleck (New York: Simon and Schuster, 1979), pp. 162–81.

[6] George Chauncey, Jr., 'From Sexual Inversion to Homosexuality: Medicine and the Changing Conceptualization of Female Deviance', *Salmagundi* No. 58/59 (Fall/Winter): 114–46.

[7] Martha Vicinus, *Independent Women: Work and Community for Single Women, 1850–1920* (Chicago: University of Chicago Press), p. 158.

[8] Sharon O'Brien, 'The Thing Not Named: Willa Cather as a Lesbian Writer', *Signs: The Lesbian Issue* 9.4 (Summer 1984): 576–99.

[9] H. Montgomery Hyde, *The Love That Dared Not Speak Its Name: A Candid History of Homosexuality in Britain* (Boston: Little, Brown, and Co., 1970), p. 1.

the potentially controversial subject of same-sex relationships which neither pedestalizes nor perverts the lives in women's texts or the texts of women's lives.

Carol Smith-Rosenberg suggests that instead of seeing nineteenth-century same-sex relationships in terms of a Freudian 'dichotomy between normal and abnormal' (p. 2), they should be viewed as falling within 'a continuum or spectrum' (p. 28) which includes at one end 'committed heterosexuality, at the other uncompromising homosexuality' (p. 29), with 'a wide latitude of emotions and sexual feelings' in between.[10] Such a spectrum enables us to see the possibilities for 'closeness, freedom of emotional expression, and uninhibited physical contact' (p. 27) which characterized women's same-sex relationships during this era. While Smith-Rosenberg is able to perceive women moving freely 'across this spectrum' (p. 29), she does not intend to obliterate the framework of a 'gay'/'straight' dichotomy. On the other hand, Adrienne Rich reinterprets and recasts Smith-Rosenberg's 'continuum' focusing almost exclusively on same-sex relationships and de-emphasizing what Rich terms 'compulsory heterosexuality'.[11] Rich explores the broadest possible spectrum of female friendships and comradeship 'including the sharing of a rich inner life, the bonding against male tyranny, the giving and receiving of practical and political support' (p. 648–9). Like Smith-Rosenberg, Rich welcomes the potential for homoeroticism within the perimeters of what she calls a 'lesbian continuum' or 'range – through each woman's

[10] Carol Smith-Rosenberg, 'The Female World of Love and Ritual: Relations between Women in Nineteenth-Century America', *Signs* 1.1 (Autumn 1975): 1–29.

[11] Adrienne Rich, 'Compulsory Heterosexuality and Lesbian Existence', *Signs* 5.4 (Summer 1980): 631–60.

life and throughout history – of woman-identified experience' (p. 648). Unfortunately, because the image of the 'lesbian' is frequently 'defined by sexual behaviour alone', many people fail to realize the point that Smith-Rosenberg and Rich want to emphasize: that 'physical love between women' is but 'one expression of a whole range of emotions and responses to each other'.[12] Therefore, with those individuals in mind who would have difficulty identifying with 'lesbian' terminology, I have chosen a more neutral term which allows for the least possible instances of exclusion.

The word 'homorelational' can be used to describe the full range or spectrum of same-sex relationships which can and do occur through each person's life. 'Homorelationality' is more inclusive than 'lesbian continuum' because it takes the attention away from sexual persuasion and focuses on gender. Hopefully, the notion of homorelationality can help eradicate some of the stereotypes surrounding homosexuality by facilitating studies of male and female same-sex relationships which investigate behaviour rather than sexuality. Also, by putting the emphasis on 'relatedness' rather than sexuality, it offers alternative ways of investigating women's and men's same-sex relationships which otherwise are all too often compared and contrasted to male/female relationships. In the plethora of theoretical speculations and semantic postulations, two realities seem to emerge: first, that relationships between women and relationships between men fulfil many women's and men's personal and public needs in ways that are uniquely different and exclusive from their relations with the so-called opposite sex; and second, that the diverse kinds of emotional bondings and social interac-

[12] Blanche Wiesen Cook, 'Female Support Networks and Political Activism', *A Heritage of her Own*, editors Nancy F. Cott and Elizabeth H. Pleck (New York: Simon and Schuster, 1979), p. 420.

tions which historically have and still do transpire
between members of the same sex are not a series of
unimportant, unrelated, or disconnected episodes but
rather part of a lifelong continuum of homorelationality.

The concept of homorelationality enables literary
biographers like myself to explore the breadth and
scope of the same-sex relationships in the autobiographical writings of nineteenth-century women such as
Ethel Arnold who lived during eras when words like
'lesbian' were not commonly used to describe their
sensations, feelings, and identification with women (p.
100).[13] Ethel M. Arnold (1865–1930) was the youngest
and only single female member of that branch of the
Arnold family tree which included such illustrious
persons as her sister, Mrs Humphry Ward, Somerville
College co-founder and novelist; her father, Tom Arnold
the Younger, teacher and scholar of English; her uncle,
Matthew Arnold, poet and essayist; and her grand-
father, Thomas Arnold, Headmaster of Rugby School.[14]
One might assume that being an Arnold would have
provided certain personal and professional advantages
for Ethel, but she frequently found herself unsupported
by a patriarchal Victorian family which focused on her
social status as spinster instead of her creative potential
as author. It might be argued that despite her flair for

[13] Joyce Trebilcot, *Dyke Ideas: Process, Politics, Daily Life* (Albany: State
University of New York Press, 1994).

[14] The first phase of my original research on Ethel M. Arnold was conducted
during 1982 when I was awarded a Summer Bursary by the University of
Tulsa's Center for the Study of Literature under the direction of Germaine
Greer. Since that time, I have returned to England on numerous occasions
to examine primary material in Oxford and London as well as to
interview family members. I am currently revising my dissertation on
Arnold (Temple University, 1984) for future publication by Macmillan
Press, London.

biography and literary criticism she didn't progress beyond the level of an inspired dilettante who dabbled in a variety of avocations from acting and photography to journalism and public speaking on behalf of woman suffrage. Nevertheless, even though her later years were plagued by financial dependency and substance abuse, Arnold's life, when viewed within a cultural/historical context, epitomizes the New Victorian Woman's ongoing struggle to achieve self-actualization, economic independence, and socio-political autonomy. Like so many of her generation, this little-known Arnold was forced to confront crises of belief, social pressures, and political issues without benefit of historical precedent.

Amidst the challenges of a rapidly changing world, one stabilizing factor for Arnold was the way in which she actively sought the companionship of other women for emotional nurturance, political solidarity, and professional mentorship. There was something unique about how growing numbers of women from all classes were beginning to collectively value their own self-worth through the formation of close female friendships. Perhaps what makes Ethel Arnold's life-story particularly poignant and noteworthy is that she was acutely aware that her loving attachments to female relatives and friends were the cornerstone of her emotional life which in turn fortified her in her quest for self-discovery, community consciousness, and artistic expression.

As women like Arnold began to explore new kinds of relationships, pursue new career opportunities, and fight to protect newly-won rights as well as seek to acquire additional protection under the law, they were starting to act out in reality the life-stories upon which the rewritten plots of the twentieth-century novel would later be based. What makes Ethel Arnold exceptional is that she was one of those New Women in transition who attempted to creatively transcend both the nineteenth and twentieth centuries through the medium of her art. By addressing some of the inner conflicts and external pressures which were shaping their protagonists' life experiences, transitional New Women writers such as Arnold were offering their protagonists new possibilities for personal fulfilment other than those of home, husband, and children. By refusing to limit their narratives to the traditional male/female roles and prescribed domestic themes which had become the hallmarks of the nineteenth-century romance, writers like Arnold could permit their heroines to entertain alternative modes of personal expression such as transvestism and same-sex bonding. By desiring to achieve greater control over their artistic choices as well as over their life processes and decisions, these transitional New Women writers were becoming the very protagonists they were attempting to create.

In an effort to accommodate these non-conventional heroines and non-traditional themes, early twentieth-century writers had to develop new kinds of story lines which Rachel DuPlessis refers to as rupturing or 'breaking "the sequence – the expected order"' (p. 34).[15] Writers also had to invent new ways to resolve their heroines' less than traditional dilemmas or what DuPlessis calls 'writing beyond the ending' (p. 5). Yet as early as 1894, Ethel Arnold was expressing in one of her book reviews to *The Manchester Guardian* a conscious awareness of those 'genuine old-fashioned love' stories, 'ending, in the orthodox fashion, to the

[15] Rachel Blau DuPlessis, *Writing Beyond the Ending: Narrative Strategies of Twentieth-Century Women Writers* (Bloomington: Indiana University Press, 1985).

tune of wedding bells' which had 'long been the staple article in the fiction market' (p. 10).[16] Rather than perpetuating the traditional images of domestic and marital bliss by imitating the 'wholesome, well-bred, sentimental' fiction written predominately by and for women, writers like Arnold were redirecting their attentions to a newer type of story which teemed with 'problems' (p. 10). By crafting a fiction for and about women which introduced new themes, plot sequences, and conclusions, late nineteenth and early twentieth-century women writers were providing a much needed vehicle for reinforcing and popularizing the image of a new kind of woman whose reality was gradually coming to pass.

If the modern heirs of the New Woman's literary legacy can more easily erect and comfortably dwell in temples of their own creation, it is because transitional figures like Arnold dared to personally, professionally, and artistically break the ground upon which new narrative frameworks could be constructed, which served as important links between traditional and modern forms. Like other previously and temporarily lost novels, Ethel M. Arnold's *Platonics: A Study* takes the reader to that place where the texts of covertly lived lives and the lives contained within covertly-written texts intersect, where fiction becomes autobiographical and autobiography is fictionalized, and where the lines separating the real from the ideal often appear virtually non-existent.

Ethel Arnold's non-traditional attitudes on same-sex relationships are fictionally depicted in her only novel *Platonics: A Study* which idealistically surveys the love

---

[16] Ethel M. Arnold, Review of *Britomart* by Mrs Herbert Martin, *The Manchester Guardian*, 9 January 1894, p. 10.

between two female friends.[17] In *Platonics*, Arnold 'studied' the interplay of Platonic oppositions, mind or reason and physicality or desire.[18] Arnold pits two diametrically opposed female characters one against the other within an innovative construct which functions much the same way as a Platonic dialogue. This dialectical framework enables Arnold to question whether a life of action and sexual passion is better than a life confined to the passive recesses of the mind. What is especially interesting about *Platonics* is that Arnold transforms a potentially didactic and static narrative into a believable story. Through economy of phrase and precision of language, Arnold crafts a plot whose fable-like simplicity provides a foundation upon which many layers of symbolic meaning can strategically and precariously balance. At the same time, she explores the ways in which each of her oppositionally-drawn female characters is able to 'relate' to a certain male interloper as well as to each other.

With a touch of unconventional daring, Arnold allows the mentally-grounded Susan Dormer and the physically-activated Kit Drummond to go through a series of connected episodes which open the possibility for both heterosexual and 'homorelational' bonding.[19]

---

[17] Ethel M. Arnold, *Platonics: A Study*. Subsequent page references to this novel will be cited in the text of the paper.

[18] According to Plato, 'then we may fairly assume that they are two (oppositions), and that hey differ from one another; the one with which a man reasons, we may call the rational principle of the soul, the other, with which he loves and hungers and thirsts and feels the flutterings of any other desire, may be termed the irrational or appetitive, the ally of sundry pleasures and satisfaction? Yes, he said, we may fairly assume them to be different' (p. 294). Jowett, translator, *Dialogues of Plato*, editor Justin D. Kaplan (New York: Washington Square, 1950).

[19] Ethel Arnold's use of the name Kit is interesting since it is ambiguous as to gender.

Their respective relationships with one another and with the third character, Ronald Gordon, do not merely serve as ends in themselves but as prisms through which the author can filter the polarity of the two female protagonists. Because of their disparate and shared experiences, Susan and Kit are able to undergo changes not only from within but also between themselves. The result is a work which attempts to candidly address the separate but related dilemmas of these two female friends: one whose seeming loss of power prevents her from expressing her emotional need to love and another whose desire for self-actualization inadvertently leads to the seeming loss of that other woman's love.

On a literal level, the novel investigates how two friends can be separated by time and circumstance. The rigid and seemingly unfeeling Susan, who secludes herself in a Castle on the banks of the Tyne, is contrasted with her beloved friend Kit whose zest for living is an inspiration to everyone who knows her. When the widowed Susan is unable to accept Ronald Gordon's proposal of marriage, he becomes enamoured of the vivacious Kit who has recently returned to England and to Susan after having been away for four years. As Ronald and Kit discover they share mutual interests, their casual relationship becomes more serious. When they announce their decision to marry, Susan passively withdraws from her two friends. While the couple are living in Venice, Susan's maid sends word that her employer is ill which prompts Kit to return to Susan's Castle. Even though Susan is unable to express the full extent of her devotion to Kit except in an unmailed letter and Kit doesn't realize the depth of her affection for Susan until it appears to be too late, a spiritual bond of Utopian love ultimately unites them.

Unlike many nineteenth-century heroines who find
their complementary 'other half' in the so-called
opposite sex, Ethel's female characters find completion
in the hearts and minds of each other. Despite the fact
that Kit's marriage temporarily distances her from
Susan, the presence of Ronald Gordon cannot hinder
the inevitability of the two friends' reconciliation. In a
sense, Arnold more than Ronald[20] exemplifies the third
component of passion in her Platonic scheme since the
author serves as the motivating force or creative catalyst
which brings the two characters to a state of holistic
completion and harmonious integration.[21] Yet while
the two women appear to merge in a higher expression
of their former closeness with Susan coming 'back to'
Kit (p. 128), it is possible that the very Platonic framework which unifies Arnold's novel may, in fact, inhibit
the two women's attainment of emotional fulfilment
within the real world either separately or together.

Certainly, the outcome of the novel might well have
been different had the author openly defied convention
and allowed Susan to put aside all thoughts of rejection
so that she could mail her letter to Kit. If Susan had
mailed that letter, Kit might conceivably have gone to
her friend's side much sooner. Yet even if Arnold had
not been restricted by her Platonic construct, there are
perhaps more significant reasons for her reticence about
reuniting Kit and Susan in the flesh rather than in the

[20] It is possible that Ronald is a transposition of the name Arnold.

[21] Plato also states that 'passion, which has already been shown to be
different from desire, turns out to be different from reason' (p. 296).
Plato concludes that when man 'has bound together the three principles
within him, which may be compared to the higher, lower, and middle
notes of the scale, and the immediate intervals – when he has bound all
these together, and is no longer many', he becomes 'one entirely temperate
and perfectly adjusted nature...' (p. 301). Jowett, translator, *Dialogues of
Plato*.

spirit. Quite possibly, Ethel was hesitant to overtly
present a fully realized same-sex relationship lest she
reveal too much about her own strong attachments to
women. For despite her efforts to veil her account of
same-sex love by focusing on the spiritual ideal of the
women's 'platonic' love, it is apparent to the modern
reader that *Platonics* is not just another Victorian
romance novel. It is not hard to believe that the author
was extremely empathetic to her female characters'
situation, especially when Kit takes 'Susan's cold, thin
hand' and presses it 'between her two strong, warm
ones' in an attempt to reassure her that despite her
plans to marry Ronald, she loves Susan first who has
been 'mother, sister, and friend' to her (p. 103). But
Ethel was aware that although her nineteenth-century
readers would not necessarily be offended by such
passionate moments of same-sex friendship, they would
neither accept nor understand an unveiled account of
two women whose love for each other 'surpassed the
love of men'.[22]

According to the critic for the *Athenaeum* (27 January
1894, p. 110), 'the real interest of the story is just
beginning where Miss Arnold leaves off. As this is
certainly a novel of the class which is dignified by the
title "psychological", we might reasonably ask that the
centre of interest should fall within the actual situation,
and not in the sequel.'[23] This nineteenth-century
reviewer's curiosity concerning what he felt was
Arnold's unfinished narrative focuses on 'whether the
course of true love is likely to run smooth' in Kit and

[22] Lillian Faderman, *Surpassing the Love of Men: Friendship and Love
Between Women from the Renaissance to the Present* (New York:
William Morrow, 1981).

[23] Review of *Platonics*, *Athenaeum*, 27 January 1894, p. 110.

Ronald's marriage. On the other hand, some twentieth-century readers, myself included, might argue that the real interest of the novel is the loving relationship between Kit and Susan. A correspondent who wrote Ethel Arnold's obituary for *The Manchester Guardian*, 10 October 1930, astutely observed that *Platonics* 'would have aroused much more attention if it had been published to-day'.[24] For when viewed within the context of the traditional fiction of the nineteenth century, the novel takes on special significance given Arnold's willingness to covertly 'study' the subject of female homorelationality.

By suggesting, if even on an 'ideal' level, that Kit and Susan can somehow resolve their dilemma through a same-sex relationship, Arnold is defiantly offering an alternative to the traditional romance which ended on a note of storybook marital bliss or else concluded much too tragically when all options for heterosexual union had been exhausted. In a way, the very appeal of a *Platonics* for this modern reader is the very tension which underlies the covertly delicate interplay between what is actually stated and what the author may have wanted to explore further or have her characters verbalize more directly

For example, the modern reader tends to question Kit's motives, for though she is far more decisive than Susan, Kit is decidedly reluctant to marry Ronald Gordon. Is it because she has only known him for a short while or that she fears the marriage could somehow affect her friendship with Susan? When Kit speaks of betraying Susan, is it because she feels guilty that Ronald is seeing her on the rebound? Surely, the

[24] Obituary, 'The Late Miss Ethel Arnold', *The Manchester Guardian*, 10 October 1930, p. 15.

unconventionally independent Kit is much too set on getting and doing everything she wants to let social protocol get in her way. Or was her former relationship to the intensely serious Susan, from whom she all too conveniently withdrew herself for four years, something other than the 'platonic' union that Ronald apparently shared with the widowed Susan Dormer? For Kit ambiguously states, 'I was a friend before I was a lover, and though I have gained you I have lost her' (p. 97). Kit then confides to Ronald that 'I shall be more and more shut out from her heart. And though I love you truly and deeply, I loved Susan first, and for ten years she has been my very life' (p. 97). It is apparent that even after Kit's marriage to Ronald, Susan is never far from Kit's secret thoughts. The narrator is quick to point out that 'there are some women whom no man's love can altogether compensate for the loss of a woman's, and Kit was one of them' (p. 109).

I suggest that instead of reading *Platonics* as an unfinished heterosexual love story or even as a heterosexual plot with a coded lesbian subplot, the novel might be viewed as a homorelational narrative in which the two women's attachment could serve as a metonymic vehicle for a 'study' of what I term 'generic love'. Generic love is a concept of loving which is neither gender-based nor gender-biased toward or against heterosexual and homosexual relationships. In such a reading, the marriage between Ronald and Kit is not necessarily inferior to the Utopian kinship between the two women since once Kit realizes that she is capable of loving and being loved through her experiences with Susan, she can only be that much more responsive to Ronald or any other person with whom she chooses to engage in a reciprocally intimate relationship. I feel that not only is the idealized love shared by Kit and Susan equal in intensity and devotion to anything Kit will ever share with Ronald, but also the women's homorelationality is a kind of model of what all love should represent. Notwithstanding such a reading, I am still of the opinion that the late Victorian critic's confusion as to what happens to Kit and Ronald's marriage is the result of the normalcy with which Arnold treats the closeness between the two women friends which at times seems to border on the 'passionate' rather than being strictly 'platonic'.

We, the modern readers of *Platonics*, might well ask why Ethel Arnold never again published another work of fiction. Was it because she believed her fictive efforts would continue to be misunderstood by the patriarchal critical community or her readership? Was she no longer able to write the 'new' kind of novel which teemed with 'problems' as it emphasized the independent New Woman and her less than conventional relationships? Is it possible that Ethel's veiled account of same-sex relationships was the verbalization of her own state of being split in half regarding her own highly repressed sexual feelings or represented a shielding of actual but secret romantic attachments with other woman? Or perhaps Arnold was unwilling to risk becoming too autobiographical in her fiction since, like Susan, she had come dangerously close to openly declaring her own preference for the company of women.

Although it may never be known whether any degree of passionate intimacy existed between Ethel and her many close female friends, the potential for its expression was certainly present. In order for the events in *Platonics* to have been so convincingly

written, some of the female characters' experiences had
to be present in Ethel's own life. No doubt Ethel was
particularly mindful of her own close friendship with
Agnes Williams-Freeman when she was drafting her
novel. Since theirs was the stuff out of which marriages
are made, it is quite possible that they shared a sort of
'Boston marriage' or long-term monogamous
relationship, especially during the 1890s when *Platonics*
was published.[25] What is known from Arnold's
writings as well as from family letters, diaries, and
gossip was that a 'continuum' of homorelationality or
same-sex relationships provided an ongoing source of
support for her which began with mother love and
adolescent crushes and progressed to a deeper
emotional commitment to various women. Although
Arnold's poetry and any private journals she might have
kept would perhaps be more revealing than her public
works, from reading *Platonics* one begins to get a very
real sense of her personal attitudes and feelings.[26]
When all conjecture is done, what is known is that
Ethel Arnold devoted one of her best creative efforts to
the exploration of how female friendships are capable
of fortifying a woman in ways which are both exclusive
of and different from a woman's attachments to and
with men.

I believe *Platonics: A Study* is a revolutionary text
because Arnold is able to view female homorelationality
through eyes that are untainted by post-Freudian
sexuality. It is quite possible that modern-day same-

[25] According to Lillian Faderman, the term 'Boston marriage' was used in
late nineteenth-century New England 'to describe a long-term monogamous relationship between two otherwise unmarried women'
(*Surpassing the Love of Men*, p. 190).

[26] To date I have been unable to locate any of Ethel Arnold's poetry since,
like her journalism, her poems may be unsigned.

sexuality will never be fully understood until people begin to accept and understand their own homo-relationality, because to view female relatedness in terms of male/female sexual relations is not to view it at all. Just as Professor R. H. Blyth speaks of poetry as 'the something that we see' in which 'the seeing and the something are one' since 'without the seeing there is no something, no something, no seeing' (p. 84),[27] so, too, must we begin to strip away those filters through which we view the world, which prevent us from perceiving and acknowledging the existence of worlds and world views seemingly beyond our ken which may, in fact, be as valid if not equal to our own.

It is remarkable that a pre-Freudian writer, Ethel M. Arnold, was able to fictionally bridge that historical moment when female loving would soon cease to be acceptable fare in either literary or real life arenas. Even today Arnold's model of generic loving runs counter to post-Freudian society's unwillingness to view the various expressions of female intimacy as fluid and natural processes of relatedness in which all women continually partake consciously and unconsciously throughout their lives. It is, therefore, fortuitous that Arnold's work which was initially misread and then conveniently forgotten should now 'come out' figuratively and 'literarily' 100 years after its initial publication in 1894. As the historian Jules Michelet observed, people (and books?) 'necessarily have to die in order to be judged and resurrected by history'.[28] In the growing canon of works being written by, about,

---

[27] R. H. Blyth, *Zen in English Literature and Oriental Classics* (Tokyo: The Hokuseido Press, 1942).

[28] Anne Seymour, 'Anselm Kiefer: The Women of the Revolution', London: Anthony d'Offay Gallery (May 1992), p. 2.

and for women, *Platonics: A Study* is indeed a significant contribution which serves as a living memorial to what it universally means to be a woman in relationship to other women.

Phyllis Wachter
Philadelphia, 1995

SELECT BIBLIOGRAPHY
OF ETHEL M. ARNOLD

Platonics: A Study. London: Osgood, McIlvaine and co., 1894.

Tourguéneff and his French Circle (Translator). Editor Ely Halperine-Kaminsky. London: T. Fisher Unwin, 1898.

Essays and Short Stories

'Edged Tools', *Temple Bar*, August 1887, 494–509; September 1887, 77–93.

'Knowledge', *Oxford High School Magazine*, April 1880, 65–7.

'Mrs. Verrinder', *Temple Bar*, June 1886, 187–220.

'Public Spirit', *Oxford High School Magazine*, July 1880, 99–100.

'Reminiscences of Lewis Carroll', *Atlantic Monthly*, June 1929, 782–9.

'Reminiscences of Lewis Carroll', illustrated. *Windsor Magazine*, December 1929, 43–52.

'Rhoda Broughton as I Knew Her', *Fortnightly Review*, August 1920, 262–78.

'Social Life in Oxford', *Harper's New Monthly Magazine*, July 1890, 246–56.

Articles and Reviews

Review of *The Amazing Marriage* by George Meredith, *The Manchester Guardian*, 25 November 1895, p. 8.

Review of *Britomart* by Mrs Herbert Martin, *The Manchester Guardian*, 9 January 1894, p. 10.

'The First Decade of Our Corporate Life', *Oxford High School Magazine*, December 1885, 901–9.

Review of *A Gentleman of France* by Stanley Weyman, *The Manchester Guardian*, 2 January 1894, p. 7.

Review of *Illuminations* by Harold Frederic, *The Manchester Guardian*, 14 May 1896, p. 10.

Review of *The Life of Professor Henry Morley* by Henry S. Solly, *The Manchester Guardian*, 15 November 1898, p. 4.

'The Marriage of Mrs. Peel', *The Manchester Guardian*, 25 April 1895, p. 5.

Review of *Memoir of Ralph Waldo Emerson* by James Elliot Cabot, *The Reflector*, 19 February 1888, 165–71.

'Mr. Asquith's Wedding', *The Manchester Guardian*, 11 May 1894, p. 8.

Review of *Murder de Luxe* by Rufus King, and *Canary Murder Case* by S. S. Van Dine, *The Manchester Guardian*, 29 July 1927, p. 70.

Obituary – Margaret Oliphant, *The Manchester Guardian*, 28 June 1897, p. 7.

'The "Photographic Salon"', *The Manchester Guardian*, 24 September 1898, p. 6.

Review of *The Pilgrimage of Ben Beriah* by Charlotte Yonge, *The Manchester Guardian*, 6 April 1897.

'The Royal Academy Banquet', *The Manchester Guardian*, 4 May 1891, p. 6.

'The Royal Photographic Society's Exhibition', *The Manchester Guardian*, 26 September 1898, p. 10.

Review of *The Spoils of Poynton* by Henry James, *The Manchester Guardian*, 23 February 1897, p. 4.

'Working Men's Clubs Association', *The Manchester Guardian*, 9 May 1891, p. 9.

PLATONICS

A STUDY

BY

ETHEL M. ARNOLD

" We, in some unknown Power's employ,
  Move on a rigorous line ;
Can neither, when we will, enjoy,
  Nor, when we will, resign."

LONDON
OSGOOD, McILVAINE & Co.
45, ALBEMARLE STREET, W.
1894

SECOND EDITION

TO THE DEAR MEMORY

OF

MY MOTHER.

PLATONICS.

CHAPTER I.

HE library at Damesworth was
a most pleasant and liveable
room.   In winter the firelight from the big open fire-
place gave it the aspect of a haven from
the keen Northumbrian winds ; in summer the sunlight falling on the dark oak
overmantel carved by Flemish hands in
days gone by, on the worn leather bind-
ings in the shelves, on the small tables
bright with odds and ends of *bric-à-brac,*

took away all sombreness and deepened the sense of human fellowship with the dead and living which all old houses bring. It was the principal living-room of the Castle, for the drawing-room was a big, comfortless room which Susan Dormer had soon decided to be "impossible," and deserted accordingly, and gradually the library had assumed that air of graceful habitation which, perhaps, only a certain type of Englishwoman knows exactly how to produce. It was nearly ten years since Mrs. Dormer had come to Damesworth as the wife of a man much older than herself, whom the detail of life had finally worried out of existence into the family vault, and for six years Susan Dormer had lived a solitary life, with no child of her own to keep her company.

She was a woman of somewhat peculiar mind and temperament. In early life she had spent herself in an intensity of devotion to her own people—particularly her mother—to one or two friends, and lastly to her husband, whom she had loved with the same quality of ardent affection she had lavished upon her family, rather than with passion. One by one they had passed away from her into the great Silence, and at each successive blow she had rebelled more bitterly and vehemently against the power which seemed to her only to create human beings in order to make them suffer. When, at length, her husband died after a long and lingering illness, she developed a morbid dread of the future, and set to work steadily and resolutely to wall up her heart against all further invasion. For the first two years after her husband's death she shut herself up more and more from the outer world, preserving as her only link with it one intimate woman friend, the solitary human being whom she loved. At

the end of the two years Kit Drummond
was called away from England by an
imperative duty, and Susan Dormer was
left absolutely alone in her grey Northumbrian Castle on the banks of the
Tyne. In her solitude she turned more
and more to books, seeking from them
first of all companionship and distraction
rather than any definite consolation.
She read an immense deal of history,
training her mind by degrees to see men
and events *en bloc,* and to distinguish
the enduring elements in human nature
under the ever-changing fashions of circumstance. From history she turned to
philosophy, reading always voraciously
and intelligently, not, as men for the
most part read philosophy in the schools,
for the sake of the mental discipline, but
in the hope of finding the absolute Truth,
not realizing that it still is where it was
originally planted—at the foot of the rain-
bow. The greater part of what she read

she probably did not understand, for the fortress of thought is not to be stormed in any such summary fashion. Still, her reading afforded her mental food and stimulant, and gradually she evolved a philosophy of her own, vaguely realized at first, but passing as the years went by into a sort of passionate conviction, taking the place of all other beliefs and hopes. It seemed to her that individualism, the imprisoning of the soul within the walls of the Ego, was at the root of all the sin and misery of the world, and that she had suffered in the past because she had nursed and fostered her individuality instead of setting herself from the first to break down the barriers which separated her soul from the world-soul. In reality it was a modern form of asceticism which derived as much stimulus from the thought of sacrificing this earthly, personal life in order to join the "choir invisible," as Christians of all ages have obtained from the hope of forming conscious part of a visible choir in Heaven as a reward for similar abstinence. The conviction grew and grew with her till it became a sort of mental anæsthetic deadening all sensibility, a sort of moral refrigerator freezing all the channels of her once overflowing affections.

But it is seldom that character is allowed to develop itself unchecked in any one direction, and it was just as Susan Dormer seemed finally to be succeeding in severing herself absolutely from her fellows that the old owner of the house across the river died and a young heir stepped in to take his place. Almost as unsociably disposed as Susan herself, though from quite different causes, Ronald Gordon, man of the world, traveller, dabbler in many things, had soon discovered that Mrs. Dormer was the only person of interest in a rather British neighbourhood, and by dint of persistent yet unobtrusive effort had at length succeeded in breaking down the barriers of Susan's reserve, and establishing himself on terms of friendly intimacy at Damesworth. Before the end of Gordon's first year at Seaton they were seeing one another almost every day, thereby causing a good deal of animated gossip in the county, and in spite of much vehement disagreement on many questions they found one another increasingly pleasant company. The months slipped by, and all unknowingly the heart which Susan fully believed to be dead awoke to a new and passionate life.

So matters stood till, at the end of four years from the time she went away, Kit Drummond wrote to say she was coming back to England.

One September afternoon tea for two stood waiting on the little straw table in the library. The wind which, light or boisterous, is never altogether wanting in Northumberland, huffled into the room through the open window and played games with the lighted spirit-lamp ; the ridiculous little clock on its stand of brass bookshelves chimed five o'clock noisily and peremptorily. A sound of voices came along the passage outside, and Susan Dormer opened the door with an open telegram in her hand, followed closely by the butler.

" Is the boy still here?" she asked, and the tones of her voice sounded pleasantly in the high-ceilinged room.

" Yes, ma'am," said the man ; " he's waiting for an answer."

" I'll write it at once," she said, and going to the writing-table she took down a telegraph-form and wrote the following message :—

"To Miss Drummond, 500, Sloane St., S.W.—Delighted to see you to-morrow morning—Susan," and was in the act of handing it to the butler when a shadow fell across the doorway.

"May I come in? What! *more* telegrams? Why, the world must be coming to an end!" said a man's voice, and a tall figure strolled lazily into the room and stood facing Mrs. Dormer on the other side of the table. At a sign from her he threw himself into the nearest arm-chair. It was Ronald Gordon, and he had come in for tea and talk after a long day's salmon-fishing. Susan waited till the man had closed the door, and then drew her chair up to the tea-table.

"Why must the world be coming to an end?" she asked, as she ladled the tea into the tea-pot.

"Because you have sent at least three telegrams in as many days, which means that you are coming out of your cell," he said, rising slowly to his feet and walking across to the tea-table.

"It means nothing of the kind," said Susan. "It means, if you wish to know, that my best friend has come back to England after four years, and is coming here to-morrow."

"Of course I wish to know," he said, his manner changing a little. "I might have known that good things can't last for ever."

"You are foolish to talk like that," said Susan, with slightly heightened colour, and handing him his tea. "Kit is my other self."

"But I don't want another you!" he burst out, putting down his cup and pacing the room with his hands in the pockets of his rough homespun knicker-bockers. "I was quite happy with one you. We've got on so well—you and I —so exceptionally well; a third person will be such a bore!"

"You forget," said Susan, "that the third person in question is my best friend."

"But surely you can see that that only makes it all the worse—that *I* want to be your ' best friend !' " he cried.

"You'd better drink your tea," said Susan ; "it's getting cold."

"Bother my tea!" muttered Gordon under his breath, but flinging himself into his chair nevertheless. "You know perfectly well that I've no friend but you —that one friend is all I want or care for."

" Well, perhaps after to-morrow you'll have two," said Susan. "Did you have any sport to-day?"

"Oh ! I didn't come here to talk about salmon-fishing," with an impatient shrug of his shoulders.

"I beg your pardon," said Susan, " but you very often do." And then they both laughed, and the ill-humour faded from his face.

As he sat with his back to the light, his candid eyes following every one of

her feminine movements, he was a striking, attractive-looking creature. There
was something a little superfine about
him—about his long, thin, nervous hands
and his look of perfect grooming, but
men who thought him so at first sight
generally changed their opinion when
they saw him in the hunting-field or
handling a salmon-rod, and there were
few women who failed to be attracted
by the combination of grey hair with a
ripple in it, dark moustache, and darker
eyes, which made him so singularly
pleasant to look upon.   Then, too, there
was something rather rare and exquisite
about him.   With a touch that suggested
decadence of class and type, he expressed
their best things too—things that are, as
it were, the flowers of the past.   If he
were a little over-bred, he had all the
fineness, the gentleness, the perfection,
in a word, which only a soil impregnated
with such traditions can produce.   His

cleverness and a distinct note of origi-
nality would under any circumstances
have made him a charming companion,
but it was his freedom from self-consciousness and that perfect humanness
which, in spite of more elaborate definitions, is all that the best civilization
amounts to, which made intercourse
with him pleasanter than with many an
abler man. With quick perception, Susan
Dormer had seen all this in him, and had
the more readily granted him the friendship which she kept so studiously
guarded from the world in general.

For some time they sat in silence,
gazing into the fire which even in
summer a Northumbrian house can
rarely dispense with, and meditatively
drinking their tea. At length he rose to
put down his cup. She looked smilingly
up at him, and their eyes met in a look
which she was the first to break.

"I am sorry I was cross just now," he

said suddenly; "but I have been very happy for three years, and that is a good deal to say. One gets to hate change and to understand the tactics of the ostrich. Whenever I think of the future I feel inclined to hide my head in the sand."

"Why think of it at all, then?" she said, with a laugh, but her face was averted, and her voice trembled more than his had done.

"Because I can't help it!" he said, moving a little away. "When one is happy one grows nervous and superstitious. Fate is so much bigger than we are, and has no preference whatever for hitting men of his own size. Still, one can cheat Fate sometimes. Don't you think we might try?"

"I don't know what you mean," she said.

"I mean that we are happy in one another's society—at least, you have often told me you like my company; and as for me, you know what I feel about yours. Well, at any time something may come between us. Why shouldn't we circumvent Fate? Why shouldn't we bind ourselves together by a bond which not even Fate can break? You know now what I mean—why shouldn't we marry?"

For one moment she looked at him sharply, penetratingly, and then her eyes dropped and her face blanched. She got up from her chair and walked over to the window, where she stood looking out upon the oval lawn and the dying northern sky.

"I thought you knew what I felt about those things," she said, presently.

"I know you don't fancy bonds of any kind," he said, laughing rather anxiously. "But we won't call them bonds; they shall be nothing but a design to cheat Fate."

"I don't mean that," she said, still

with her back turned towards him.   "I
thought you knew that I had made up
my mind never to marry again."

"You have implied as much," he said;
"but it is difficult to believe in things one
doesn't like.   I've been trying to per-
suade myself that I might induce you to
change your mind.   Won't you let me?"
and he moved towards her.   She turned
and faced him, and the light behind her
hid the pallor of her face.

"No, you cannot change my mind,"
she said.   "You cried out against change
just now, and yet you wish to make the
greatest one of all.   We will be friends—
always—nothing more."

His face saddened as she spoke.

"I am desperately sorry," he said.
"I suppose I had let myself hope.
Won't you tell me why, and then I
won't bother you any more?"

"Yes, I think I can tell you why,"
she said, motioning to him to sit down

and doing so herself; "but I doubt if you'll understand." There was a moment's pause, after which she began to speak in a slow, expressionless tone.

"We have often discussed theories of life and conduct—you and I," she said, "and as often as we have discussed them we have agreed to differ. You believe in the intensification of each moment of individual life; you are a modern of the moderns, for to you Time holds Eternity in its folds, not Eternity Time. From such a view of life mine is as far as the Poles asunder. Every hour of my life of late years has taught me more clearly that form of any kind is the one thing that passes away—that personality, individuality, *self,* in a word, perishes, that the universal remains. To me the one thing that is abidingly real is not this self of mine, this 'bundle of desires and activities,' but the general

C

life from which my life-current came, to which it goes."

"I totally disagree with you!" he exclaimed; "but——"

"I know you do," she broke in quietly, "and the disagreement is vital. Believing as I do with all my mind in the necessity of self-obliteration, how can I form ties which could only delay the process? Convictions may be rare nowadays, but they have not lost their strength."

He stood looking down upon her gravely and a little perplexedly. Since the moment when she had turned her back upon him and walked over to the window she had become a different being. Then she had seemed warmly, pulsatingly human, and he could feel the individual life which she repudiated so strenuously throbbing and beating in her. Now she had become cold, ascetic, remote; the very lines of her face had

changed, and her smooth paleness
matched the even monotony of her
voice.

"I don't understand such a philosophy,"
he said at last; "it seems to me cold,
inhuman, repulsive. The fact is, you are
a mystic out of date, and should have
lived in the Middle Ages. I feel dread-
fully lonely and cut off from you. Does
it come within your scheme of things to
make other people miserable?"

Her only answer was to burst into
tears. In a moment he was kneeling at
her side, murmuring words of self-
abasement.

"Forgive me, forgive me—you are so
much to me; let us forget and be friends
again. It has been so sweet, this friendship of ours; if it mayn't be more, let it
at least be unchanged. I am not worthy
of more. I know it so well, but don't
cut me adrift altogether."

She rose to her feet, and laying her

hand on his shoulder, she stood looking down at him through her tears.

"There are some things which nothing can change," she said, with quivering lips. "You have come into my life—it can never be quite the same as if I had never known you. Isn't that enough? If I have hurt you, I pray you to forgive me, and I beg of you to leave me now."

He bent low over her hand, and the next moment he was gone.

She stood for a moment looking at the door through which he had passed, while the tears gushed quietly, swiftly, from her serious eyes. She felt stifled, and everything in the room seemed to mock her. What meaning have civilized surroundings when the heart is aching? The crucible of one single human emotion can reduce all life's paraphernalia to ashes. Brushing the tears from her face, she went quickly out of the room, down the broad low stairs, across the sombre old hall, out of the front door into the evening light. Over the park lay the grey dusk in which the cattle moved restlessly and dimly; overhead the clouds trailed in thin orange-coloured bars across the windy sky; beyond the broad, swift-running river the lights of Seaton shone with a steadfast glow. Up and down the terrace she paced, short hurrying gusts of wind ruffling her hair and sighing round the keep, till dusk had deepened into darkness.

It all grew terribly clear to her on that chill autumnal evening. The work of years was all gone, swept away, destroyed by one rush of passionate emotion. Her philosophy had failed her in the hour of need. All it had been able to do for her was to lend its formula to her lips, for the better concealment of what she had suddenly realized to be dwelling in her heart. And in this moment of absolute self-revelation she knew that if Ronald Gordon's feeling for her had been love instead of liking the formula would have gone too. She felt as if she were struggling in deep water and could find no foothold. The years to come confronted her in harsh, unlovely guise. Had it all to be done over again, then, that slow, laborious deadening of the heart?

The gong sounded for dinner; she heard it through the open windows, and seeing the figure of a servant standing on the morning-room steps, she signed to him that she was coming. Once more she turned and looked across at the lights of Seaton.

"You called me cold and inhuman," she cried, flinging out her arms in the darkness; "but if you had loved me you would have understood, and it might all have been different."

And then she went in to the lonely, lighted house.

CHAPTER II.

T seven o'clock next morning, while the sun was still chasing away the early morning mists and resting on the shining grass, a carriage drew up before the fine old Jacobean porch of the Castle, and a tall, slender, heavily-cloaked girl sprang out on to the steps. A wide-brimmed straw hat, rough tweed clothes covered almost entirely by a shepherd's plaid Inverness cape, a soft white shirt with a stick-up collar a little crumpled with travelling, business-like brown boots, and corduroy gaiters made the whole figure essentially modern-looking, and every one of her quick, alert movements spoke of long habits of self-dependence and self - management. Stopping a moment in the hall to pick up the letters which lay waiting for her on the table, she walked quickly across to the swing-door, pushed it open with one vigorous movement of her hand, and taking the low stairs two at a time, was at the top in the twinkling of an eye and knocking at Susan Dormer's door. A low cry sounded from within, the door opened, and the two friends, separated so long, were together once again.

"Come here to the light, that I may look at you," said Kit Drummond, drawing Susan towards the big sunny bow-window after the door was shut and they were safe from all intrusion. "I want to be sure it's really you. Yes," she went on, after a moment spent in drawing Susan down by her side upon

the window-seat and scanning the well-loved face with her long green eyes;
" you are still my Susan ; but you look tired, dear heart. What have you been doing ? "

" I didn't sleep much," said Susan, a faint colour tinging her pale, austere face ; " that's to say, I only fell asleep about five, and that's how I came to be up here instead of downstairs to welcome you. Put your arms round me as you used to do, Kit. I am tired still, but so glad to have you again that nothing matters now," and her head drooped wearily on to Kit's shoulder.

Holding the frail, slight figure in her strong, young arms, bending over the small head and whispering loving, soothing words into her ear, there came a look into Kit Drummond's face which few people would have believed it capable of —a look of such tenderness, such benign loving-kindness, as almost raised friend-

ship into a sacrament. She knew that
something was wrong, but she knew
not what, nor cared so long as she might
help and comfort

"Susan," said Kit, at length, "I think
the best thing for you to do will be to
get back to bed while I go and tub; then
I'll come back and we'll have breakfast up
here together. I feel travel-stained."

"Very well, but don't be long," said
Susan, freeing Kit, who stood up and
thrust her hands deep into her pockets
with a sigh of content and well-being.

"My dear, I can't be limited as to
washing after a night-journey," she said.
"Besides, I've been four years camping-
out, and I forget what a bath-room looks
like," and she went laughingly through
the door, across the library to a large
cheerful room on the other side of the
house, which was always kept for her
and called by her name. It was all
exactly as it had been on the day, four

years ago, when she had bade good-bye
to Susan and started to join a brother
in the wilds of Canada. They were
alone in the world, she and the brother,
and he had wanted her and she had gone
—for six months, as she thought at
first. But the six months lengthened
out into four years, and now he was
married and needed her no longer, and
she had come back. That was the whole
story, and a very commonplace one in
the world of women.

At the sight of each familiar object in
the room—the little silver box of biscuits
on the table by the bed, the blue table-
cloth with the looking-glass spangles on
the round table in the middle, the cheerful chintz curtains, the bright fire, the
mullioned windows framing the little
chapel in the park, and the distant grey-
green Northumbrian hills — her heart
seemed to melt within her. It was indescribably sweet to be back, indescrib-

ably soothing, indescribably consoling. Yet, as she slowly took off her things, one thought detracted from her perfect content—the memory of the look in Susan's eyes, a look of pain deep and abiding, underlying all her joy in Kit's return.

It was nearly an hour later when a washed and rejuvenated Kit Drummond presented herself at Susan's door and demanded admittance. The maid was busily spreading out the breakfast on a small table by the bed in obedience to Mrs. Dormer's directions. To poor famished Kit it looked a very attractive repast indeed, and without further delay she drew up her chair to the table.

"Susan," she said, as the door closed upon the maid, "when I tell you that I have lived for the past twelve hours upon one pre-historic bun, you may, perhaps, pardon my emotion at the sight of eggs."

"My poor dear!" said Susan, laughing. "Set to work at once, and don't
talk. I'll content myself with looking at
you."

But half of her friendly injunction
passed unheeded, for though Kit did full
justice to her breakfast, she was certainly
not silent, and the time passed quickly
by as the two friends picked up the
pieces of the past four years.

"And your neighbour at Seaton?
What of him?" said Kit, after many
questions had been asked and answered.
"Do you see as much of him and find
him as pleasant as you did at first?"

"Yes, we are very good friends,"
said Susan, while her eyes turned from
Kit and fastened themselves upon the
foot of the bed. "I want you to know
him, and thought of asking him to dine
to-night. Should you mind?"

"Of course not," said Kit, though her
heart sank a little at the thought of any

third person disturbing their first evening together after four long years. "I
suppose he fishes?"

"Oh, yes, he fishes," said Susan, and
silence fell upon them both. To Kit as
she sat at the bedside with her hand in
Susan's, looking at her every now and
then with a quick, keen glance, one half
of the situation at least became clear.
What about the other half? That she
had still to find out, but the strained
look in Susan's eyes made her uneasy.
Soon they fell to talking again, but more
constrainedly ; their intimacy seemed
less full and perfect than before, and Kit
felt chilled. She was struck, too, by
the extraordinary isolation of the life
Susan Dormer seemed to have been
leading, and it repelled her a little.

"Have you had no one at all to stay
with you of late?" she asked.

"No one since you went," said
Susan.

"And that is four years ago!" exclaimed Kit. "You never cared much for the general run of your fellows, but isn't that carrying the dislike too far?"

"I dislike no one," replied Susan; "but I've been trying to do without people. Hav'n't I spoken about it in my letters?" she asked, a little wearily.

"Every now and then you have talked about some such ideas," said Kit, rising and walking over to the window, "but I never took you seriously."

"Why not?" said Susan. "You would have taken me seriously enough if I had told you I had joined the Church of Rome. Are there no other convictions possible?"

"Of course," with an impatient shrug of her shoulders; "but no amount of conviction can alter the fact that you're a human being."

"No, but it can affect my view as to the destiny and meaning of human beings—and it does," and she looked coldly across at Kit.

Kit met the glance by one of searching scrutiny. Something had puzzled her in Susan Dormer's face ever since she had arrived. Possibly this variety of mental weed she had just described, grown and cultivated in solitude, lay at the root of the matter. And as she looked at her, at the thin, nervous face, the lined forehead, the sad, strained eyes, the pity of it impressed her very painfully, and it came into her mind with what absurd arrogance the men of action air their blood-and-thunder definitions of life, and how each soul works out the drama of existence with equal intensity, whatever the *mise-en-scène*.

"Susan, darling," she said, going over to her and bending over her, "your theories are all very wonderful and apparently complete, but you have left out one thing which upsets all your calculations—your own very human heart. It has upset many philosophies — and philosophers—in the past ; it will upset more in the future. Sixthly and lastly, why don't you marry Ronald Gordon ? "

Startled by the suddenness of the question, Susan Dormer looked up sharply and half-suspiciously into her friend's eyes ; but there was something so reassuring in their smiling affection that she was disarmed, and her look softened.

" You are very like yourself," she said, putting up a hand to stroke Kit's face.

" That's no answer," with a protesting shake of her head.

Conscious of her persistence, Susan dropped her hand and half turned away.

" Surely I must often have told you my views about marriage," she said, shortly.

"Oh! I'm so tired of 'views'!" cried Kit.

D

"Can't you be human for one little moment and answer a human question?"

There was a moment's pause, during which Kit walked to the window and buried her face in a bowl of late roses.

"Ronald Gordon asked me to marry him yesterday," said Susan Dormer, at length, in an altered voice, "and I told him that, feeling as I did about human ties and relationships, it was out of the question. Will that satisfy you?"

For a moment Kit did not look round; when she did, her eyes were blazing.

"No!" she cried, "it won't satisfy me at all. Shall I tell you what I think about it? I think it's the most complete specimen of nineteenth-century morbid, distorted stuff and nonsense I've ever heard of, and——"

But Susan put her hands before her face as though to shield herself from the torrent of Kit's excited words.

"Don't say any more," she said, while her voice shook. "What I've told you is quite true, but—he doesn't really love me, and that is the root of the matter. I would rather not talk about it any more."

The next moment Kit's arms were round her, and the shadow that had come between them melted, for the time being, altogether away.

The rest of the day passed somewhat slowly to both the two friends. For, in spite of the re-establishment of confidence between them, they were both conscious of a new element which had come into their lives, disturbing the whole delicate fabric of their relationship. And, as always happens under such circumstances, the perfect ease of friendly intercourse was marred, and, for the first time, a touch of self-consciousness affected them both uncomfortably. During what remained of the morning

D 2

Kit occupied herself with a general over-
hauling of her fishing-tackle, and a long
conversation with the fisherman as to
the prospects of sport, while Susan
Dormer, after having dispatched her note
asking Mr. Gordon to dinner, and receiving his answer in the affirmative, settled
down into a state bordering upon apathy,
and resisted all Kit's efforts to rouse or
amuse her.   In the afternoon Susan's
ponies came round, and Kit, taking her
old place on the box-seat of the Moray
waggon, took her silent companion for
a long, aimless drive across the high
bleak uplands. The heather, which is
always scanty, had browned earlier than
usual, giving a touch of autumnal
sombreness to the delicate neutral tints
which characterize the Northumberland
moors. Overhead, the sky was a soft
blue, greyed and shadowed by a faint
sea-mist ; rolling away to the horizon,
line after line of rounded hills passed

through every shade of yellow from tawny orange to palest saffron, and in the thin sunlight every blade of the rough moorland grass which clothed their sides seemed distinct and individual. It is a country with none of the breathless beauty of the Highlands, but its wide and still expanses give to the ' cabin'd spirit' a grateful sense of space, and the romance which dwells still in hill and valley gradually sinks deep into the heart.

With the exception of a few stray remarks about the weather or the view, a heavy mantle of silence lay upon them both as the ponies bore them rapidly along the rough hill-roads. Both were busy with their own thoughts, and both availed themselves of the privileges of intimacy to the full, and when at length they found themselves once more at the Castle, Kit entered it with a feeling of unaccountable depression very different

from her gay, excited entrance of the
morning.

It was some minutes after the gong
had sounded when Kit Drummond made
her appearance in the library that evening.
Ronald Gordon had arrived, and was
standing with his back to the door, talking to his hostess, but at the sound of
Kit's rustling gown he turned, and for
one brief moment his eyes met hers—
the next, he was being formally introduced by Mrs. Dormer. For the first
time in her life Kit had no small talk
ready, and after shaking hands with him,
she moved aside to the table and stood
absently fingering the day's newspapers,
while everything in the room seemed to
whirl a little and a sort of buzzing sounded
in her ears. " It's living so long in the
backwoods, I suppose," she thought to
herself, " that makes me so ridiculously
disturbed at meeting anybody ;" and
when, a moment later, dinner was an-

nounced, she found herself mechanically moving downstairs, still tongue-tied, and with a sense of unaccountable shyness upon her.

The dinner was not a very brilliant success. Susan Dormer was constrained and for the most part silent, and not even all Ronald Gordon's *savoir faire* could make the three-cornered conversation anything but spasmodic and fragmentary. Towards the end Susan gave up all further attempt to talk, and fell into an abstracted musing, and a Wagnerian discussion arose between Kit and Gordon, which, though it led to no decision of vital import to the world, yet served to isolate them both, and surround them with a common interest, unshared by Susan, who cared nothing for music. And when, later on, the two women passed from the room, leaving Gordon to his cigarette, Kit was full of that curious feeling of exhilaration which is

born of accidental contact with an unex-
pectedly congenial mind.

In the library the firelight glowed
welcomingly, and the two friends drank
their coffee standing on either side of the
wide fireplace, while the light accen-
tuated the pallor of the one and the
tremulous brightness of the other.

"He is an interesting man," said Kit,
moving off to the piano.

"Yes, he has used his eyes and his
ears," said Susan, taking up a book, and
dropping into her favourite chair. "Are
you going to play?"

"Yes, I think so. Do you mind?"

Susan half turned, and there came a
flash of her old gaiety into her tired eyes.

"Aren't you a little like 'Uriah Eap'
to-night?" she asked. "Don't ask any
more foolish questions, but play all the
things I like."

So Kit began, and soon the room was
full of curiously intense, throbbing waves

of sound.. There was no method in
her playing ; it was as individual as the
rest of her. People of correct musical
taste and no musical instinct shuddered
when she played Beethoven's Sonatas
with variations by Kit Drummond, or
versions of nocturnes by Chopin, or
romances by Schumann, such as the
composers themselves had certainly
never dreamed of in their wildest
moments.

Still there was a spell in it, a sort of
compelling power over her instrument
which seemed to make it speak as she
willed and what she willed, and in the
end it conquered most people. To-night
she was wandering in spirit in her
beloved Highlands, the land of her birth
and of her traditions, and pibrochs and
reels and love-songs followed one another
in a wild confusion of sound. In the
midst of it the door opened, and Gordon
passed noiselessly to a chair whence he

could watch her, though unseen himself. The tumult of notes fell for a moment, the heavy-lidded eyes dilated and burned, and the first notes of "Annie Laurie" sounded through the room. He put his hand over his eyes and listened, and as the melody of the beautiful old song rose and fell, he seemed to be out upon a stretching purple moor, with the west wind blowing in his face, and the scent of the heather in his nostrils, and walking with him, talking to him, was a woman with disturbing, magnetic eyes.

She rose from the piano and came over to the fire, holding out her foot to the blaze. There was a heavy silence in the room. Presently Gordon's hand fell to his knee, and at the same moment Susan threw down her book and pushed back her chair, while a wave of colour passed over her face.

"Surely it's very hot to-night," she

exclaimed. "My head is bursting," and she rose, and going over to the window, parted the curtains and looked out. Kit took the opportunity to slip from the room, while Gordon joined Susan at the window, and the two stood looking abstractedly out upon the looming trees and the cloud-barred moon.

"I think it's time for me to go," he said, presently. "You're evidently both tired, and *you* look very white," he added, looking at her with friendly anxiety. "Have I stayed too long and talked too much?"

"Neither," she said, while she passed into the lighted room again, "but I am wretched company to-night. Well, are you sorry she came?" she added, with a wintry smile, stopping him under a tall standard lamp which barred the way.

"No," he said, while his eyelids quivered a little under the directness of her gaze ; " you were quite right, as you always are. She is charming."

" She is going to fish to-morrow. I think you'd better go down, too, to keep her company," she said, still looking at him.

" Very well," he said, moving away from the bright light, " but I can't get down till latish. And now I will go. Good-night," and he held out his hand with a smile.

" Good-night," she said. " I will say your good-byes to Miss Drummond. I think she is over-tired," and she moved towards the bell while he passed quickly from the room. The next moment he came back. She was standing as he had left her, only her head had fallen forward a little, and her hand hung by her side.

" Did you call me ? " he asked, stepping hurriedly towards her, struck by something in her attitude.

She looked up at him, but her eyes were unseeing. "No," she said, "I didn't call.   Good-night."

He stood for a moment irresolutely, but seeing that she meant dismissal he went reluctantly away, leaving her alone once more.

CHAPTER III.

HEN the two friends met at breakfast next morning there was a certain air of fatigue perceptible about them both, but the sense of restraint seemed lessened, and they talked freely. Kit had already donned her fishing-skirt and wading boots, and clumped about during the meal with a truly sportsmanlike tread in quest of buttered eggs and tea-cake and other breakfast commodities.

"I don't much like the look of the weather," said Susan, as they rose from the table. "There's been a perfect water-spout in the west, and I shouldn't wonder if the river came down in the course of the day. Do be careful," she added, looking anxiously at Kit, who was busily soaking her casts at a side-table.

"Oh, it's all right," said Kit. "Robson knows the river by heart. Besides, I don't think it will be down before the afternoon, anyway."

"Well, I'm glad Ronald Gordon will be there, too," said Susan, bending down over the basin in which the casts lay soaking and examining them with a sudden and unwonted curiosity.

"Is he going to fish to-day?" asked Kit, without looking up, while the fingers which manipulated the gut paused a moment in their work. "He didn't say anything about it."

"Yes, he did; just before he went away last night," said Susan; "but most probably he won't be down till towards the end of the morning. He'll be at the Straits, below you. And now I must go and order dinner," she added, drawing herself up. "Good luck to you, my Kit," and she stooped and kissed her.

Kit flung her arms round her. "Won't you come down some time this morning? I shall be lonely without you."

"Pooh!" retorted Susan, disengaging herself. "You know perfectly well that when you've a rod in your hand you are dead to all human feeling. Still, I will come if I can," and she went smilingly out of the room.

The sky certainly looked uncomfortably sullen and beetle-browed when, twenty minutes later, Kit emerged on the terrace. Robson was waiting for her with her fishing gear, and at her appearance he went quickly forward and opened the gate in the park railings.

"What do you think of the weather, Robson?" she asked, as they walked

clumsily along in their waders over the
cattle-cropped grass. "Will the river
come down?"

"I shouldn't wonder if she did, miss,"
said Robson, in his soft Northumbrian
burr. "She's a bad collour, and there's
been a grëat deal of rain over yonder.
You'll not have much sport to-day, miss,
I'm afraid."

"Oh, well, we must hope for the
best; there's nothing so unexpected as
a salmon," and she laughed one of
her healthy, fresh-air laughs. "How
familiar it all looks!" she added, half
under her breath, stopping for a moment
to look round her: at the Castle standing on the ridge behind them, grey and
square against the dense background of
the turning beeches; at the low hills in
the distance with their thin belts of
wood; at the old folly across the river
which rushed over the rocks below
them. She felt stirred and moved by it

E

all, and it was with a sigh of complex
feeling that she strode on once more.
Nevertheless, Susan Dormer's accusation
proved to be more or less true, for the
fisherman's passion finally routed all
other emotions, and by the time she
had reached the river-bank she was
lost in an uneasy contemplation of the
clouds massed in the west and of that
grey look in the water which is so full
of ill-omen to the angler. There was
evidently not a moment to be lost, and
choosing a brightish fly after some little
consultation with Robson, she took the
light fifteen-foot greenheart rod in her
small, strong hand, and waded knee-
deep into the ashen water.

Close into the opposite bank the stream
ran swift and deep, and a hundred yards
further down the water began to break,
falling a little lower still in a heaving,
tumbling mass over a ridge of rocks into
a deep, swift-running pool below.   It

was the first of the three Damesworth
salmon casts, and when the water was
in order it could hardly be beaten along
the whole length of the river. But to-
day no coaxing, nor skill, nor persever-
ance seemed likely to bring the fish to
the fly. Three times Kit fished it down
with neat and careful casts, leaving no
part of the stream unfished, but though
twenty-pounders jumped in maddening
numbers all round, they were clearly
only doing it "to annoy," and not one
of them paid any attention to her fly.
At last she handed the rod over to
Robson with a gesture of impatience.

"Put on a brighter one still," she
said, as she waded to shore; "that
is the only chance. I'll fish it down
once more, and then give it a rest."

After a few moments spent in the
change of fly, a new and brilliantly
seductive object dangled at the end of
the cast, and with a laugh and a shrug,

she once more entered the water and
began casting as before. For some
minutes she remained stationary, letting
out a little more line each cast in her
endeavour to get the fly well across to
the opposite shore. Suddenly an intent
look came into her face.

"One more over there, Robson," she
said, in a low, excited voice to the
keeper, who stood leaning on the gaff
close to her. "I think I felt a touch,"
and as the fly swung round with the
stream she lifted it neatly from the water,
and with a long, clean cast dropped it
close into the opposite bank. There was
a moment's breathless pause, and then a
great boil in the water and a sharp
whirr ! from the reel, and Kit was fast in
a heavy fish. For a minute or two he
seemed overcome with surprise at this
sudden interference with his liberty, but
not for long ; a sudden tug, which sent
Kit's heart into her mouth, seemed to

apprise him of the gravity of the situation, and with a bolt and a rush he was off down stream, while the unfortunate fisherwoman tumbled and scrambled after him as best she could. With a great effort she managed to steer the fish clear of the rocks, where she would infallibly have been broken, but that was all she could do, and before she had time to take breath she found herself on the edge of the deep water below, holding on for dear life. Everything depended on the next few minutes, for if the fish were still determined to go down stream, she would almost certainly lose him, for the bank below was thickly wooded, and the wading was too deep for her, and she had, consequently, nothing but length of line to depend upon.

"You can put on a little more strain, miss," said Robson, who was watching the fight with breathless interest; "you must take it out of him somehow."

Nodding her head, she began slowly to reel in, and for a moment or two she met with little resistance, when *whirr!* went the reel again, and the fish was splashing in the shallow close into the opposite shore. For fully twenty minutes he pursued the same tactics of short and sudden rushes across and down stream, but Kit kept as heavy a strain upon him as she dared, and at length he began to roll a little and show signs of exhaustion.

"You can bring him in now, miss," said Robson, straightening himself up, gaff in hand; "he's aboot tired out."

And so it proved, for though, once or twice, as Kit drew the fish steadily into shore, he made a fresh struggle to free himself, he was evidently played out, and at the end of another five minutes he lay like a bar of silver on the bank.

"It couldn't ha' been done better, miss," said Robson, as he brought out his steelyard and slipped the hook into the mouth of the fish. "Fourteen pounds and a quarter!" he added, holding it up for her to see; "and as bright as a spring fish."

For a minute or two Kit stood proudly surveying her prize and surreptitiously rubbing her left arm, which was aching a good deal, though she would have suffered torture rather than confess it. Then she turned round and looked searchingly down the river.

"Isn't there someone fishing at the Straits, Robson?" she asked.

"Yes, miss," said Robson, his eyes following the direction of her gaze. "It'll be Mr. Gordon."

"I wish you would go and see if he's had any sport," she said, as she strolled towards the fishing-hut a hundred yards up the river. "I shall rest for a few minutes, and then try the same fly down again."

"Very good, miss," said the man, and after putting down the rod close to the hut and depositing the fish in a safe place, he moved away across the grass.

The hut was very comfortable, her sense of physical fatigue very strong, the view framed by the hut-doorway very peaceful, and as a result of so many combined influences not many minutes had passed before Kit was fast asleep, and she was just dreaming that a salmon of incalculable size was dragging her down the river at the rate of sixty miles an hour, when a voice said, apparently close to her and quite à *propos*,—

"That's a fine fish of yours!" and she opened her green eyes wide upon the tall, slight figure of Ronald Gordon standing in the doorway of the hut.

"It's a minnow compared with the one I've just been dreaming about," she said, laughing. "I'm so thankful you woke me up—it was bigger than a whale. Have you had any sport?"

"None whatever," he replied; "moreover, I've broken my rod, and Robson is helping my man to mend it. You don't mind his stopping down there for a few minutes, do you? I can look after you just as well, you know," and his smiling eyes seemed to take friendly possession of her.

" I don't think you realize how independent I am," she said, smiling back at him as she sat lazily curled up in her corner. " It's true I can't gaff my own fish, but then, as I'm not in the least likely to get another, that doesn't matter, does it?"

" A sentiment at once cheerful and desponding," he said, with a laugh. " But do you know," he went on, after an anxious look towards the west, " I think you'd better fish while you can; we sha'n't have much more time. But perhaps you're tired?"

"Oh, no," she said, jumping to her feet; "I must fish the stream down once more," and she took her rod from its resting-place. "Did you ever see such a fly?" she said, holding out the gaudy object between her finger and thumb for his inspection as they walked across the stones to the river's edge together.

"It's your best chance," he said. "On a day like this one has to resort to fascination. Where are you going to begin—here?" as they stopped at the brink.

She nodded, and stepped into the water, while he followed closely after her.

"I am going to wade rather deep just here," she said, "because the fish are lying well over to-day."

"All right," he said; "I'll keep a little ahead so as to make it quite safe for you," and he stepped past her. As he did so the wave he made in the water shook her balance, and she was on the point of falling when he quickly put out a hand to steady her.

"I'm *so* sorry," he said, still holding her hand while she regained her footing; "it was idiotic of me to pass you as suddenly as that. Are you quite sure you're all right now?" he added, as she drew away her hand.

"Perfectly," she said, with a smile, while the slight vibration in his voice made her heart throb; "the stones are rather slippery to-day."

For the next few minutes they were both silent, he walking slowly on ahead, while she followed, casting every two yards, and so absorbed were they in what they were doing that a distant rushing sound behind them, which increased steadily in volume, either passed altogether unheeded or formed merely a sort of accompaniment to their thoughts, and before either of them had time to realize what was happening, a great solid wall, fully three feet high, of thick and muddy water came rushing round the bend of the river.

Up at the Castle the hours slipped by quickly enough to Susan, and she had got through all her housekeeping and all her accounts and business-letters, besides an hour's reading, by half-past twelve. As the clock chimed the half-hour she put down her books with a sigh, and stretching her arms over her head, she looked out across the park. In the west the clouds had fallen lower and lower, till all the distant hills were blotted out. A vague nervousness seized hold of her. She thought of Kit, and her heart awoke to life again with a sense of pain and anguish. She threw open the window and leaned out. A man's figure came in sight, mounting the ridge which sloped down to the river-bank. He was moving very quickly, and as she looked more closely she saw first that he was running, and then she recognized that it was Robson. With a sudden fear clutching her heart, she caught up her hat and cape, and running quickly down the stairs, she came out on to the terrace just as he ran breathlessly up to the gate.

" What is the matter? " she asked, in her shortest, most peremptory tones.

" The river came down of a sodden, m'm," he panted out. " Miss Drummond——"

" Is drowned ! " she broke in. " Oh, *why* did I let her go ! " and she clung to the railings, staggering.

" No, no, m'm," he said, with a dull sense of having given unnecessary pain. " She's not drowned, but she fell down and hit her head against a stone and is just stunned, and they're waiting till she comes to."

" Where are they ? " said Susan, straightening herself up and passing through the gate.

"By the hut at the rocks, m'm," he said. She started to run across the grass.

"Tell Frazer to go for the doctor," she said, turning round for a moment, "and then follow me down."

A few moments later she found herself nearing the river-bank, and not a hundred yards from her lay Kit with Gordon bending over her, while his man was filling his hat with water at the edge of the hugely-swollen river. She went noiselessly up to them and touched Gordon on the shoulder.

"Let me come," she said, with a touch of coldness in her voice; "it is my place."

He lifted his head, and, seeing it was Susan, moved silently away.

"Yes, of course, it is your place," he said. "She has been like this ever since the fall, about a quarter of an hour ago. There is some slight concussion of the brain, I think. Thank God you've come."

"How did it happen?" she asked, in a low tone, laying her cool hand on the girl's white forehead, and bending over her for one scrutinizing moment.

"I hardly know," he replied, in the same tone; "the whole thing was so sudden. She was fishing, and I was walking on ahead to test the wading for her. If it hadn't been for that, I think I must have heard the river coming. But you know how sharp the turn is just there; one's only chance lay in one's ears, and when one is *in* the water one's ears are deadened. There was just one moment left to get out in, and we managed to scramble ashore somehow, independently of one another, when suddenly she staggered, and before I could reach her she fell back on to the rocks, striking her head rather badly. Luckily, it was a smooth bit of rock, so her head isn't cut. She seems to be merely badly stunned."

"Where was Robson?" asked Susan.

"Down below at the Straits, helping my man to mend my rod, which was broken. The whole thing was a chapter of accidents, for if he'd been with us it would never have happened. Of course, directly afterwards they both came running up, for the flood had reached the Straits."

She nodded her head, and for a few minutes there was no sound but continuous roar of the river over the rocks. Both were absorbed in the unconsciousness of the girl. The whiteness of the face seemed to accentuate the beauty of its oval lines, the stillness of it to harmonize like sleep with the balanced tranquillity of her being; the strange penetrating charm which affected those around her like some subtle melody hung about her, binding the silent watchers to her beautiful life by cords made of their heart-strings. To the man she seemed like the realization of some half-forgotten dream, dreamed when the world was young ; and as he watched, life lost its mystery and complexity, and straightened out into the broad pathway of love.

At length the eyelids fluttered and opened, and the tender eyes looked out once more upon the world they loved ; a faint smile hovered into them at the sight of the two bent heads, and then they closed again. But the worst was over, consciousness had returned, and the rest was only a question of time.

Soon they were able to carry her up to the Castle on a shutter which the thoughtful Robson brought down with him from the house, and she was put gently into bed. Later on the doctor came, ordered rest and quiet, and was generally encouraging, and Susan left the

F

room soon after his departure in order to give his report to Gordon, who was standing by the hall-fire vainly endeavouring to dry his clothes and still the chattering of his teeth.

"She will be all right in a few days," she said. "There is no cause for alarm of any kind, and now, please go and change at once. I sent over for some dry clothes directly we came in, and they must be here by now. I let you do as you wished and wait till Kit was settled because I don't believe in thwarting people at such times, but now you must really go and change. Frazer will look after you."

"Oh! I shall be all right," he said, pushing open the swing-door with rather a shaking hand. "Thanks so much for thinking of me at all. I don't deserve it, since the whole thing was my fault. I will change and go straight back if you won't mind letting me have a trap."

"I would rather you stayed to dinner," said Susan. " We shall both be anxious, and anxiety is always better shared."

" Are you sure it won't bore you to have me?" he asked, still standing in the doorway.

She turned away.

"Please go and change," she said, shortly.

He laughed, the door swung to, and she stood a moment listening to his footstep on the stairs.

CHAPTER IV.

HE growth of intimacy knows no laws. Sometimes it springs straight into maturity and seems to tell of intercourse in some former state, where all preliminaries have been gone through. Sometimes it is as gradual as the development of a flower from its seed. As Kit's convalescence merged more and more into her normal health, and she came downstairs and wandered about the grounds, Ronald Gordon came every day to inquire after her, and the two passed many hours in each other's society; and every day the intimacy,

which with them had been instantaneous, seemed to take on some added sense of stability and depth. Susan buried herself more and more in her books, and withdrew herself steadily, but gradually, from her old close intercourse with them both. Day after day she would saunter out with them into the park, or down to the river, which was still in flood, but after a few minutes of triangular talk she would invariably stroll away on some pretext or another, leaving them together.

One day the three were sitting after luncheon in the little overgrown summerhouse at the end of the terrace. The heavy clouds of the past fortnight had rolled altogether away, and the autumn sun fell on the close-mown grass of the lawn below them, and on the yellowing trees scattered across the park. Kit lay in a long garden-chair with her hands clasped above her head, looking up at the soft blue sky and the hills across the river rising to meet it.

"I should like to have a picture of this view," said Gordon, leaning forward on his stick.

"Why?" asked Susan, getting up to pin back a recalcitrant spray of honeysuckle which barred her vision. "Isn't the view itself better than a thousand pictures?"

"In itself, yes," said Gordon; "but when I look at anything like this that is beautiful and familiar, my impressions seem vague and blurred. I can't take it all in; my eye is distracted by detail, so that one moment I am thinking of, seeing nothing, but one tree; at another moment I am absorbed in the study of one particular cow. A picture appeals to one's sense of beauty distilled by memory into a pure essence. If Constable were alive, and I could get him to paint this bit of the park for me, I should feel every time

I looked at the picture a shock of feeling keener, because less diffused, than the impression I am conscious of now."

Both women cast quick, furtive glances at him from under their eyebrows. He was not often either priggish or commonplace, and when, as now, he was both, their subtle feminine instinct told them that he must be finding himself on very thin ice indeed. Neither of them spoke for a moment, and then Susan jumped to her feet with her usual abruptness.

" Well, personally, I shouldn't care if all the pictures in the world were burnt so long as the things themselves remained," she said ; " but then I am a Philistine. I'm going into the village now," she added.

" Mayn't I come with you ? " asked Gordon.

" No, thank you. I'm going in and out of cottages, and you would be sadly in the way," and she walked away across the terrace, swinging her stick as she went.

Gordon began making patterns in the gravel with his foot, while Kit lay still.

"I'm not quite happy about Susan," she said, at length. "Is it possible to do without people altogether as she is trying to do?"

"No," he said, shortly; "it is impossible."

"I try to understand it," she went on, "and I can't. To me nothing is of any real importance in the world compared with the joys and sorrows, the hopes and fears, of human fellowship. I would exchange every gift in the world for the genius of loving."

A sudden light came into his eyes, and his hand closed tightly upon the arm of his chair.

"Do you find most people interesting?" he asked, a little abruptly.

"In a broadly human sense, yes," she answered. "At one time I thought I could only like clever people; then I thought I could only like well-bred people; and so on through many phases of limitation. Now I look less for the limitations in people than for the common human nature. Artificiality is the one barrier left that I can't surmount. If only people would learn that everyone can afford to be *himself*, life would be so much simpler!"

He made no answer for the moment, but the light in his eyes grew brighter.

"I like you to say those things," he said, suddenly; "they go with the fresh air and the sky, and make me feel as if I had known you always. Have you realized," he went on, bending towards her, "that three weeks ago we had never met? And now," he added, in a lower tone, "I can't imagine the world without you."

"One gets to know some people so quickly," she said, turning away her head. "No, it isn't only that," he went on, while his voice shook; "it is that you are the only woman in the world to me, the being I have waited and hungered for all my life. I felt it vaguely the first moment I saw you. I knew it when I carried you up the river-bank that day, hardly knowing if you were dead or alive. Kit"—going over to her and taking her hand—"don't turn away from me, but listen to me. I love you ; you are my very life ; it had to be ; sooner or later I had to meet you. Look at me— speak to me—I want to see your eyes, to hear your voice."

She turned her face slowly towards him, moved by a will stronger than her own ; her eyes looked up at him through narrowed lids, telling him all that he longed to know, and he hung over her spellbound, till, kneeling by her side, his arms enfolded her, and their lips met in a kiss which swept away all sense of separateness, and fused their spirits into one.

Suddenly the tears rushed to her eyes, and with a half-sob she fell back into her chair, burying her face in her hands. The thought of Susan had come back to her through a mist of happiness, and her words spoken in the bedroom on that first morning sounded again in her ears : "He doesn't really love me, and that is the root of the matter." She shivered, and shrank further into her chair.

"What is it? What are you thinking about?" he whispered, trying gently to draw her hands away.

"I'm thinking of Susan," she said, dropping her hands and looking up at him.

He rose abruptly and walked to the other side of the summer-house, and stood leaning against the doorway. His

face had a tense look, and his hands
were working restlessly.

"What of her?" he asked, presently.
"Is she to come between us?"

A sudden jar ran all through Kit's
being, the first he had ever given her.

"Don't talk like that," she said,
hastily; "it hurts me. I hardly know
how to say it," she went on, "but it
weighs on me like a nightmare, that all
this time I've been disloyal to her without knowing it. I ought never to have
come."

"What do you mean?" he said, his
fear of he hardly knew what making his
voice sound almost rough. "Mrs. Dormer
cares nothing for me nor for my actions,
but she loves you, and would like to see
you happy."

"Yes, I know," said Kit; "but Susan
told me when I first came that——"

"That I had asked her to marry me,
and that she refused me—yes, that is

so," he exclaimed, turning sharply round so as to face her. " I had meant to tell you, but since you know, there is no need to say anything further about it. We are, and always shall be, I hope, very good friends."

" Perhaps if I hadn't come it would have been different. You might have learned to love one another. Susan would be happier married, and it breaks my heart to feel that I may have come between you and her."

" Kit," he said, going over to her side again, " let me tell you the truth ; we ought to be frank with one another. I asked Mrs. Dormer to be my wife because I liked her extremely, and found her pleasanter company than any woman I knew, and because I had given up hoping to find—*you*. She refused me because she didn't care for me, and also because it is against her principles to marry anybody. And now I have found

you, we belong to one another, and no
one can come between us. Kit, my Kit,
smile at me again as you did just now,"
and he tried to draw her towards him.

But she sprang to her feet, putting out
her hands and gently pushing him away.
His words had brought no comfort to
her, for she knew Susan's heart. But
how could she betray another woman's
secret? She wanted to be alone, to
think it all over away from the thrill of
his presence and his voice.

"It may all be as you say," she said;
"but I feel confused and perplexed about
it. Susan has been my other self for
ten years. I would cut off my right
hand rather than be disloyal to her in act
or word. I would even sacrifice my
love and my hopes of happiness."

"And mine too?" he asked, a little
bitterly. "Must my life be offered up too
on the altar of friendship?"

She looked at him for a moment with

parted lips and wet, shining eyes. Then she held out her hands to him, and he took them and held them in his.

"I *love* you," she said, "and I would like to give you my life. But you don't understand. I have spent ten years in learning to be a friend, and to feel that at the eleventh hour I have failed cuts my heart."

He stood holding her hands for a few moments, closely scanning her face.

"I think I *do* understand," he said, at length ; "but remember the ruin of two lives is a good deal to weigh against the maintenance of a rather fanciful standard of friendship. If you give me up for Susan's sake, you will do no good to anyone, and you will wreck my life and yours. If you were to go away, as I see you have it in your mind to do, you could not bring Susan Dormer to care for me nor me for her ; we are not made for one another."

She drew her hands away and looked out across the river. She felt as though she were caught up and tangled in the web of circumstance.

"I don't know what to think," she said; "I am utterly perplexed. I must be alone for a time, and then, perhaps, I shall see my way more clearly. Tea must be ready, and I think I'll go in."

"Very well," he said; "I won't come with you now, but I may come again this evening, mayn't I?"

"Of course," she said, and held out her hand. He took it without speaking or attempting to go nearer to her, and they parted, walking away in opposite directions.

Susan was sitting at the tea-table in the library when Kit came in a few minutes later. She looked tired, and Kit noticed again how thin and worn she was.

"I wish you would give up that

village work for a bit, Susan dear," she said, as she drew her chair up to the table. "I'm sure you're not up to it just now."

"My dear," replied Susan, "it doesn't tire me more than other things. Life is a mistake under any circumstances, but it needn't be a *squalid* mistake. I can't bear the people on my land to feel squalid; it's unnecessarily degrading. But what did you and Ronald Gordon talk about after I left? More nonsense about pictures being better than the things pictured?"

"Oh, no!" said Kit, with a laugh; "a little of that goes a very long way. It's only when one's very young that one cares to discuss ideas of that sort at any length. After twenty-five one prefers to discuss one's neighbours."

"Does that mean you were discussing me?" asked Susan.

Kit turned away to put down her cup

G

before Susan could see the colour rush to her face.

"I never 'discuss' you with anyone, she said, shortly; "I should have thought you knew that."

"I was only chaffing, my dear," said Susan, throwing herself full length on the sofa. "Aren't you rather literal to-day?"

Kit made no answer, but went over to the sofa and laid a rug over Susan's feet. Then she sat down by them and lifted them on to her knee.

"Susan," she said, leaning over towards her," you have found me a good friend these ten years, haven't you?"

"A perfect friend. I couldn't have done better if I had designed you myself," said Susan, smiling.

"I want you to be serious for a moment," said Kit; "I've got something to say to you. If ever it should seem to you in the future as though I hadn't played a friend's part with you, try and think the best of me. I'm not thinking of anything definite," she went on, forcing a laugh, as Susan's face blanched; "but I'm morbid to-night, and trying to forestall every contingency Fate may have in store. I used to think one could absolutely control one's own life and one's own acts, but I have come year by year to realize that we're not much more than puppets. All I want to be sure of is that if at any time my movements seem to you odd and unnatural, you will know that Fate is pulling the string— not I. Will you promise me?"

Susan held out her hand in silent response to the yearning look in the girl's face.

"You could never be anything but a friend to me," she said; "it would be against your nature. Don't let's talk about that any more; it depresses me. Kit dear," she went on, after a moment's

pause, during which she seemed to grow
whiter still, " come closer to me. I too
have had something on my mind to tell
you for some time past. I've a sort of
idea that when we were talking that first
morning I gave you an impression I cared
about Ronald Gordon. If I did, it was
quite a mistaken one. I wasn't quite
sure the day that he asked me to marry
him whether I cared or not. I was
excited at my convictions being put to
the test, and I was filled with the sort of
emotion some women must feel when
they go into a convent. I mistook, in
fact, the pang caused by a general renunciation of all that most women hold
dear in life for the pang of a particular
renunciation of an individual. But it has
all cleared itself up to me now, and I
know that I didn't, and couldn't, care for
Ronald Gordon in that way. I like him
extremely, and find his company very
pleasant ; but when I told him I couldn't

marry him, I told him the absolute truth. He never more than liked me on his side, so it's all just as if it had never been. Do you understand, my Kit?" and she looked smilingly into Kit's searching eyes.

" Yes—I *understand*," said Kit, rising to her feet and walking towards the door unsteadily, for she could scarcely see for blinding tears. " I'm going to lie down for a bit before dinner," she added, as she closed the door behind her.

Left to herself, Susan pressed her hands to her eyes for one brief moment, as though her eyeballs ached. " Thank God that's over," she said to herself. The thin face fell back upon the cushions, and before many minutes were over she had fallen into a deep sleep born of utter invincible fatigue of mind and body.

CHAPTER V.

RONALD GORDON did not turn up in the evening as he had suggested, and Kit thought she understood the reason, and felt grateful to him for staying away. But though there had undoubtedly been a large element of consideration for her in his decision, there was a certain amount of egotism in it too, of which Kit knew nothing. The fact was that the presence of the two women made him feel rather ridiculous, and there was nothing he disliked so much as ridicule —self-ridicule most of all. As it turned

out, he might just as well have gone, for
Susan went to bed before dinner with
an acute attack of neuralgia, and Kit's
ministerings being neither required nor
efficacious, she was alone all the
evening. But these are the things we
never know till too late ; the obvious
lesson of which is that it is invariably
wiser to swallow one's pride and follow
one's inclinations.

In the morning, which, though
ushered in by a damp autumnal mist,
ultimately turned out fine and sunny, he
strolled down to his side of the river to
see if it were fishable. As he stood
critically surveying the colour and height
of the water, his keeper came up and
asked if he wanted to be put across.
He hesitated a moment, having fully
believed when he started out that he
had no intention of going across until
the afternoon, and being unwilling that
the delusion should be dispelled too

easily. Then he resigned himself to the inevitable, and was put across.

The grass was soft and springy, the air pleasant and the sun warm, and his spirits rose as he mounted the ridge just above the river. On reaching the top the sight of a woman's figure in the distance, bending low over the bank of the little stream which ran through the park, made his heart give a thump against his side, but on looking more closely he saw that it was Susan.

"Good morning," she called out to him, lifting herself, trowel in hand, into an erect position as he came up to her. "I can't shake hands; I'm so grubby."

"What, in the name of fortune, are you doing?" he asked.

"Planting daffodil bulbs," she answered. "I bought 3000 the other day, and am going to plant them every one myself, which means that you can do

some for me now that you're here," she
added, with a laugh.

"But I don't know how," he said.
"I never planted anything in my life."

"Then it's high time you began," she
said. "If you watch me for a few
minutes you'll soon see how it's done,"
and she turned round and set to work
again with her trowel.

"I thought you were coming up
last night," she said, presently, without
looking up. "I think Kit was disap-
pointed."

"Isn't that rather invidious?" he said,
with a nervous laugh.

"Oh, as for me, I was laid up with
neuralgia, and couldn't even see Kit."

"I am *so* sorry," he said ; and the
pang caused by the knowledge of the
wasted evening made his voice un-
usually full of feeling. "Are you better
now?"

"Quite better, thank you, as they say

up here. All the same," she added, putting her hand to her head, "I don't think this stooping is very good for me, and I'm afraid your lesson in gardening will have to be postponed. Suppose we stroll down to the river? I rather want to talk to you this morning."

"By all means," he said, with a sort of flat alacrity. "Shall I carry your implements, or will you leave them here?"

"Oh, they'll be all right here," she said, looking round over her shoulder. "Put them down on the edge by that bush, will you? Will the river fish to-day?" she asked, as they moved away together.

"Hardly; at least, it would only be an off chance. Are you making for that bench?" he said, pointing to a seat close to the water's edge. "Because, if so, I'll put a mark in and we can see if it falls while we're there."

She nodded her head without speaking, and till they reached the seat both were silent.

"I wonder," she said, as they sat down, after a journey to the brink of the river to put in the mark ; "I wonder if we know each other well enough for what I am going to say to you."

He shot a keen, apprehensive glance at her out of the corner of his brown eye.

"I imagine we understand one another and that is the chief point," he said.

"Yes, that is the *chief* point," she said, slowly, with her eyes fixed on the hurrying water. "Still, there are some things which it is difficult for any woman to say to any man."

"Anything that you could have to say to me could only be conventionally difficult," he replied; "and I don't fancy we either of us care much about conventions."

She heaved a sigh of relief.

"I hoped you would say that," she said. "Well," she went on, after a moment's pause, "we've always been very good friends, you and I, and, except for one moment of aberration, when your natural love of change got the better of you, we've never thought of being anything more or less. We have seen a great deal of one another; hardly a day has passed without our meeting, and though I suppose most people have thought us very unconventional, that hasn't affected us one jot, because we thoroughly understood one another."

"That is all perfectly true," he said. "But what is your drift? Surely, at this point in our friendship, you're not going to adopt rules and regulations you don't believe in?"

"For myself—no," she said, turning so as to face him. "But for the last three weeks I've not been alone."

A dull red tinged his usually pale cheeks and settled in his close-set ears.

"Does that make any difference?" he asked, while his breath came rather quickly.

"Not to the world, nor to myself," she answered; "but for the third person herself I cannot answer—have no right to answer."

"You surely don't mean to imply——" he burst out, after a moment spent in fiercely biting his moustache.

"I mean to imply nothing but what I have said," she broke in, quietly. "As I said just now, for myself it has never mattered, because we understood one another from the first, and I knew," she went on, speaking very slowly and distinctly, "that there was no danger for either of us; but you have been a great deal with Kit lately, and she may not have understood so well. I have been watching her very carefully, and I think she likes you. Her peace of mind is dearer to me than my own. Do you understand now what I mean? I believe you do, though," with a laugh that had a suspicion of a sob in it, "it sounds terribly as if I were asking you your intentions!"

"There is no need to say any more," he exclaimed, jumping to his feet and looking down upon her. "I should have told you soon, any way, of course; but it was difficult. Now you have made it easy. I fell in love with Miss Drummond the first moment I saw her. I mean to ask her to be my wife."

She too got up, but as she did so she reeled, and was forced to lean against the bench for support.

"I am so glad," she said, holding out her hands to him. "I hope you will forgive me for saying anything about it. Of course I suspected it"—her lips breaking into a fleeting smile—"or I should hardly have spoken. I hope you will be very happy. You must live your best life if you are to be worthy of her."

"I know it," he answered, gravely, taking her hands in his. "You may trust me to do my best." He bent down and kissed her hand. "God bless you!" he said. "I owe it all to you. How can I ever thank you enough for having shown her to me?"

She bit her lip and turned away.

"We won't talk about thanks," she said. "I think you will find Kit in if you go up to the house now. I'm going to stay here for a bit; the air does my head good."

"Isn't there anything I can do for you?" he asked.

"Nothing," she said. "I would like you to go to Kit now." And with a joy in his face he could not suppress, he walked rapidly away up the river bank.

She waited, looking steadily at his departing figure till he was lost to sight. Then she sank down again upon the bench, and buried her face in her hands.

*　　*　　*　　*　　*　　*

Ten minutes later Ronald Gordon entered the library, where he had been told Miss Drummond was to be found. She was sitting half-buried in a vast arm-chair, and so absorbed was she in her own thoughts that she did not hear him come in, and it was only when he stood actually in front of her that she looked up with a start and saw him.

"Kit," he said, kneeling down by her, "there is nothing to come between us any more ; Susan has sent me to you herself."

But she did not answer, and seemed to shrink away from him rather than to welcome him.

"Kit," he went on, trying to take her hand, "don't you understand me? I have seen Susan this morning, and she told me to come to you. She wants us to be happy."

"Yes, I know—I know," she broke out, with sudden passion, while the tears welled into her eyes. "I *know* she wants us to be happy, and we will do our best, but I was a friend before I was a lover, and though I have gained you I have lost her."

"What do you mean?" he said. "Marriage with me need make no difference to your friendship with her?"

"Not in the ordinary sense, I know, but she will draw more and more into herself as the years go by. I shall be more and more shut out from her heart. And though I love you truly and deeply, I loved Susan first, and for ten years she has been my very life."

A look of pained perplexity came into his face, and the sight of it checked Kit in her flow of excited words.

H

"Dear—my dear!" she exclaimed, "don't let's talk about it any more. I hate to make you unhappy; and if I am more conscious to-day of the pain of losing Susan than of the joy of gaining you, you must be patient with me—do you see?"

He drew a low chair up to hers.

"As you will, dearest," he said, bending towards her and taking her hand; "but don't let yourself dwell upon that side of it too much. It will only end in your getting morbid and seeing things all crooked."

She made no answer, but sat silent for some minutes with her hand in his, looking into the heart of the fire.

Then they went on to talk of other things, and the time passed quickly to them both till the gong sounded for luncheon. A message from Susan was brought to the effect that her neuralgia had come on very badly again; that she had gone to bed, and did not wish to be disturbed until the late afternoon. So the two lunched together in solitary state, and in spite of Gordon's presence and the air of devotion with which he surrounded her, Kit felt very sad and sick at heart. For hers was a radically simple nature, a nature which took people and things pretty much as she found them, and, since it looked for no complicated problems to solve, generally found none. It had never occurred to her that she might one day find herself so situated that it was impossible to take a step in any direction without hurting someone she loved. Yet this was the position she was placed in now, and life seemed very hard and uncompromising. She was tenacious by nature too, and things went very deep with her, and she knew quite well that she would never be perfectly happy in her love for Ronald Gordon. For she

had seen through Susan's words of the
night before in a moment; she knew
only too well the nature and extent of
the sacrifice Susan had made for her.
She knew, too, that there was but one
thing for her to do—to accept it as
loyally as it was offered. Still it seemed
strange and almost monstrous that this
great new happiness which had just
come into her life should be for ever
tinged with the heart's blood of her
dearest friend. Poor Kit! She had yet
to learn that whatever else might come
under that wondrous category of "in-
alienable human rights," the right to
happiness certainly does not.

She spent a strange, dreamlike afternoon with Ronald in the library, while
he told her things out of the past, and
pointed her to things in the future. But
her ear was all the time alert to catch
any movement in the room across the
passage, and her heart was aching as it

had always ached in sympathy with Susan's. Five o'clock came, and she gave him tea and sent to know if Susan would have any, but a message came back in the negative. Seven o'clock came, and she told him it was time for him to go. He asked if he might come again in the evening.

"Not to-night," she said; "I want to be at hand in case Susan needs me."

"Is it permitted to me to be jealous of Susan?" he asked, with his hand on the door-handle.

She laughed a sad little laugh. "No, it is not, and never will be," she said; "that would be the last straw. Good-bye till to-morrow."

He came back to where she was standing, and took the tall, slight figure in his arms.

"I won't say good-bye, even till to-morrow," he said; "I will only say good-night. So good-night, my beloved

—my Kit," and for a moment he held
her close. Then he stooped and kissed
her, and was gone.

She lingered in the library till the
sound of the hall-door shutting told her
he had left the house, and then, crossing
the passage softly, she opened Susan's
door and looked in.

At first the light was so dim she could
distinguish nothing, but soon, her eyes
growing accustomed to it, she saw
something dark outlined against the
window. Shutting the door noiselessly
behind her, she moved across the room.
Susan was lying along the window-seat
with her head on her hand, looking out
with wide eyes upon the growing darkness. She turned her head and smiled
as Kit approached her.

"I am better," she said, holding out
her hand.

Kit took it and, falling on her knees
beside her, laid her cheek upon it in

silence. Presently Susan, shifting her hand under Kit's chin, lifted the face up closer to her own, so that she could just see her eyes in the waning light.

"Hav'n't you something to tell me?" she asked, in a low tone.

"Yes—that's what I came for," said Kit, and though her look was trusting, it was full of a mute appeal. "Ronald Gordon told me to-day that he loved me —and I—I told him that I—loved him. But oh, Susan!" she went on, taking Susan's cold, thin hand and pressing it between her two strong, warm ones, "if it's to make any difference between us two—if you're to love me less or to live your life apart from mine, I will give it all up. I couldn't bear it. I loved you first, and for years you have been mother, sister, and friend to me. Nothing in the world, not even this strange new feeling which has sprung up in my heart, transforming life, can alter my love

for you. Tell me you will be the same
to me—that nothing can break the bond
between us."

The tones of Kit's voice seemed to fill
the room with quivering feeling. But
Susan made no answer, only turned
away her head and looked out again
across the park, while her hand lay
passively in Kit's.

"There is no reason why anything
should ever come between us," she said
at length. "It is not like that. But I
am not the same woman I was when
you first knew me. I have lived so
much alone, and dwelt so much upon
certain aspects of life, that what at one
time were merely empty theories with
me have now become convictions. You
talk of the bonds which bind us together,
but I no longer recognize bonds of any
kind. I am in a state of waiting, and
my heart is dead. I look out upon the
grass and the sky, and I long to lay down

this burden of individual life and merge myself in the World-life. There are times when I seem to break down the prison-walls and escape into the open. Don't seek to bring me back. The return to individual consciousness is like the return to life of a drowning man—an agony whose bitterness no one can know but those who've felt it. I can face it no more. Why should you cry, dear Kit?" she went on, as two hot tears fell down upon her hand. "The world is full of possibilities to you, outside and beyond my individual life. Live and love and be happy—and leave me to find my Nirvana if I can. My capacity for feeling is at end."

Kit rose slowly to her feet and laid Susan's hand gently back upon her lap.

"If it must be so, it must," she said, with trembling voice. "I can only take you at your word. But it seems to me that you are mentally ill. You may get worse or you may get better. If the latter happens, you will know that you have been ill; if not, you will never know, and I shall lose hold of you for ever. But of one thing I am quite certain—we are not born into this world to shirk life, but to live it. Somehow or other we've got to go through the whole gamut of experience, and in the end, perhaps, we shall know why. The capacity for feeling has to *grow* like everything else, shone upon by the sun of joy, watered by the rain of tears. 'I am—therefore I suffer and am glad' is a saner view of life than, 'I am— therefore I will cease to be.' But there is no need to say any more ; we speak a different language. Only remember that if ever you should want me, Susan, I shall be by your side."

Susan turned, and their eyes met. Over the white, worn face of the elder woman there passed a sort of spasm, and then an expression of utter passivity settled down upon it, smoothing out all the lines and hiding the human spirit underneath. To Kit, as she stood there, face to face with the friend of her inmost self, it seemed as if something impalpable but impassable had descended between them, wrapping Susan away into a land whither she could not follow her. With a half-sob she bent and kissed her, and then turned and left the room.

A few days later she left Damesworth for London.

CHAPTER VI.

CONCLUSION.

N the early spring of the following year Kit Drummond and Ronald Gordon were married. Susan was not present at the wedding, nor did she send any word. At first, after leaving Damesworth, Kit had written persistently once or twice a week as she had always been accustomed to do, but, her letters remaining as persistently unanswered, she had given up writing in despair. It was clear to her that Susan had meant what she said, and that for the time

being, at all events, their friendship was
at an end. Feeling totally unable to face
life at Seaton under such circumstances,
she had persuaded Gordon to let it for
a time, and for the first year of their
married life they wandered about the
Continent, stopping in out-of-the-way
places, and getting to know one another
more perfectly every day because of the
isolation of their existence. As far as
she could be happy, Kit was happy. She
was genuinely in love with the man she
had married ; she found him delightful
company, and was never bored by him.
But there are some women whom no
man's love can altogether compensate
for the loss of a woman's, and Kit was
one of them.

Autumn had come round again, the
second since those weeks at Damesworth,
and Kit and Ronald were in Venice.
They had dropped down from the Enga-
dine, over the Maloja Pass, stopping a

few days, on the way, at Promontonio,
that they might bathe in the shade of
the chestnut trees, and enjoy to the full
the sensation of standing on the threshold
of Italy—one of the few sensations
whose germs of satiety seem sufficiently
concealed. And now they were in
Venice, and the time passed like a dream
—to Kit a dream filled with vague fears
and longings.

One night they were sitting drinking
their coffee outside the hotel, waiting
for their gondola to come round. A
waiter came from the lighted doorway
into the warm darkness, carrying some
letters on a tray. Throwing the end of
his cigarette into the water, where it
fizzed for a moment and went out,
Gordon took the letters, and, after one
glance by the open window, handed
them to Kit.

"They are for you," he said.

As he put them into her hand a

sickening presentiment of evil came over her, and she sat for a few moments holding them in her lap and staring out over the water. Then she rose to go in.

"I will read them indoors, and then join you again," she said, touching him on the shoulder as she passed. "Wait here for me;" and she passed into the hall, stopping a moment under the hall-lamp to look at the envelopes of the letters she held in her hand. One bore the Damesworth postmark, and was written in a strange hand.

"I knew it," she said to herself; "I knew it," and scarcely knowing how she got there, she found herself upstairs in the sitting-room, tearing open the envelope. The letter was from Susan's maid, and ran as follows:—

"DEAR MADAM,

"Mrs. Dormer has been taken seriously ill with a heart-attack. She has had several attacks in the last two years,

but this is the worst one. The doctor
has been here this afternoon, and says
she may die at any moment. I don't
know whether I am doing right in
writing to tell you, but I feel as though
I couldn't help it—so please excuse.
She won't let me telegraph for you, but
I know she is thinking of you and wants
you. I went in just now and found her
with your photograph in her hand, and
the tears pouring down her poor thin
cheeks. She turned her head away as I
went in, and asked me to bring her
pencil and paper, and I think she is
writing to you. But when I asked her
if she wanted me to post a letter for her
she said 'No.' But, oh! ma'am, I can't
bear to see her like this any longer—so
weak, and so lonely, and so unhappy.
You may not get this in time to see her
alive, but, at any rate, I shall have done
my best, and the doctor says she may
linger for a week yet. I am sending

this over to Seaton for them to post it there.

"Yours respectfully,

"JANE THOMPSON."

Kit turned the letter over and looked at the date at the top. It was October 1st, and this was October 8th. It had followed them from Promontonio, and was a week old! It fell from her hand to the floor, and lay there with its phrases staring up at her in all the terrible legibility of a servant's hand. So it had come to this at last. Susan was dying—was even already dead— who could tell?—and she had not sent for her. Never for one moment had she lost the conviction that sooner or later Susan would send for her. And now the hope was gone, the conviction annihilated, for Susan was dying, and had sent no word. It was monstrous— unthinkable. . . .

The door opened, and Ronald Gordon

I

came in. Kit was standing in the same place where she had read the letter; it seemed as though she could not move.

"What is the matter?" he asked, going quickly forward at the sight of her face. "You have had bad news. What is it?"

"Susan is dying," she said, while her breath came in quick, short gasps— "may be dead by now."

He looked down, and seeing the letter at her feet, was on the point of picking it up, when he stopped suddenly, throwing an upward glance at her.

"Yes, you may read it," she said, with a sob. "It is only from Thompson —not from Susan. To the last she has shut me out."

He picked it up and read it, and putting it silently on the table by her side, he looked at his watch.

"We can just catch the night train," he said. "Are you up to it?"

"Of course," she answered, putting her hand to her head. "I will leave Foster behind to pack and follow us to-morrow. How long have we before we start?"

"Exactly an hour."

"I'll go and put on my things, then," she said, "while you pay the bill," and she passed out of the room, while he stood silently holding the door open for her without looking at her or offering to touch her.

At the end of forty hours' incessant travelling they found themselves, in the chill of an autumn morning, nearing the little station of Damesworth. Kit had begged Gordon to buy no papers on the way, and no telegram had been sent to announce their coming, at her special request. "I will know nothing till I reach the house," she had said. As they slowed into the station the Castle came into view on the left-hand side of

the line, but Kit knew it was coming,
and sat looking out of the opposite
window.

"Don't let anyone speak to me here,
Ronald," she said, hurriedly, as they
drew up at the deserted platform. "I'll
walk on up to the house while you take
the bags to the inn."

He nodded, and helped her gently from
the carriage. The station-master came
up, touching his hat, and seeing that he
looked communicative, Ronald took him
aside while Kit went through the wooden
gate out into the road. She walked
rapidly along, looking neither to the
right nor to the left, only passing on
her way one solitary cart laden with
turnips, whose driver gazed at her with
stolid curiosity, till she reached the gate
of the Castle. It stood wide open, fixed
back against the wall, and the soft mud
at the entrance was marked by many
wheels. At the sight of the marks Kit

swayed and half fell on to a low wall to the right, and for a moment she sat still trying to pull herself together. Then she got up and walked stumblingly down the drive as far as the sharp turn leading to the front of the house. Here she stopped again for a moment to take breath. One more step and she was in full view of the Castle. At the first glance she saw that the blinds were not down, and the next moment she found herself standing on the rounded steps of the porch, pulling the bell, and looking through the glass door into the hall.

Everything seemed as usual. A straw hat of Susan's lay on the table in the middle, and a bowl of chrysanthemums stood at either end. At the sight of the flowers her heart leapt within her, but on looking more closely she saw that they were withered. A noise sounded from within, and a sleepy-looking man

came to answer the bell. It was Frazer,
Susan's old and faithful butler. For a
moment he stopped to peer through the
glass at the unexpected visitor, and then
cautiously opened the door.

"For God's sake, let me in, Frazer!"
said Kit, thrusting herself through the
opening, and pushing past the man into
the hall as far as the table.

"You, Miss Drummond!" he cried,
calling her by the name he had always
known her by. "*You!* I'd no
idea——"

She turned and faced him, leaning
back against the table with her hands
pressed to her heart underneath her
heavy cape.

"How is your mistress?" she asked.

"She died on Monday, ma'am; she
was buried yesterday," he said, while
the tears stood in his eyes.

"*My God!*" she said, and would
have fallen, but Gordon, who had come

in quietly behind Frazer, caught her in his arms.

"Is Mrs. Dormer's maid still here?" he asked, in a low tone, as he half-carried Kit to an arm-chair by the empty fire-place.

"Yes, sir," answered the man.

"Go and tell her to come here at once," said Ronald, and the man disappeared through the swing-door. Ronald knelt down by the arm-chair and took Kit's hand in his. But she made no movement in response. Her face was rigid and her eyes staring ; she was trying to take it in that Susan was dead. The swing-door creaked on its hinges, and the maid came noiselessly up to them. Seeing her, Ronald leant towards Kit.

"Thompson is here," he said. "I will leave you with her."

At the sound of the closing door Kit half roused herself, and her eyes fell on the black-gowned figure in front of her.

" You said she was writing a letter to me," she said. " Where is it?"

" I have it here, ma'am," the maid answered, handing her a thick letter in the familiar blue envelope. " She told me I was to be sure and give it into your hands when you came."

Kit took it and held it under her cloak. " I want to go to her room," she said, sitting up. " Is it left as it was?"

" Oh, yes, ma'am," the woman replied; " it is just the same. Shall I go with you?"

" No, thank you," said Kit, and she rose heavily from her chair and walked towards the door leading to the main staircase. The maid hurried across and threw it open for her.

" I would rather not be disturbed," she said, as she passed through the door on to the stairs.

"Very good, ma'am," said the maid. "Pardon me, ma'am," she added, moving a step forward. "Was my letter delayed on the way?"

"Yes, for a week," answered Kit; "it was wrongly addressed."

"Mrs. Dormer didn't suffer much at the end, ma'am," the maid went on.

"I would rather not hear anything more, please," said Kit.

"I beg your pardon, ma'am," said Thompson. "I thought maybe you'd like to know," and she turned away.

"Yes, of course. I understand—but not just now," said Kit, and she began slowly mounting the broad, low stairs. At the top she paused a moment, dazzled by the flood of morning light, which poured in from the window across the landing. Then she opened Susan's door, passed within, and shut it carefully behind her.

The room was exactly as she had last

seen it, save that there were no flowers
in the wire flower-stand. The chintz
curtains over the bed were unchanged,
and the writing-table looked as orderly
as it had always looked, except that the
little gilt travelling clock had stopped.
Susan's favourite books stood in the
revolving book-case by her particular
arm-chair ; her sticks hung from the rack
by the door. Kit moved across to the
window-seat where Susan had lain on
the evening of their last talk together,
and falling on her knees before it, she
laid her face upon the cool chintz-covered
cushions, remembering that formerly it
had rested upon Susan's hand. For
some minutes she remained motionless,
till, sinking into a sitting position, she
took the letter from beneath her cloak
and looked at it.

It was addressed, in pencil, in Susan's
clear handwriting, to " *Mrs. Ronald
Gordon,*" and the unfamiliarity of its

look reminded Kit that it was the first time Susan had ever so addressed her. She broke the seal and took out the three closely-written sheets which lay within, and as she did so something fell on to her lap. She picked it up, and saw that it was an old faded photograph of Susan and herself, taken together soon after they first met. For the first time her lips quivered as she kissed it gently, lingeringly, and laid it face downwards upon her knee.

The letter was dated October 1st, 189—, and as Kit spread it out on the window-seat, the sight of the small, almost scholarly writing which had once been one of the commonest sights of her life filled her heart with a sudden poignancy of pain. And this was what she read, with wide tearless eyes fixed on the paper, and the tones of Susan's voice sounding in her ears:—

"KIT,—It is six o'clock in the evening

and I am alone in my room, face to face
with Death.   The doctor has just been
to tell me I may die at any moment, and
I know that he spoke the truth.   When
he told me, with that shrinking dislike
they all have to pronouncing the death-
knell of a fellow-creature, my first feeling was one of relief.   I have been so
ill these last three years that I am weary
of physical pain.   But, next moment,
my heart melted into an inexpressible
longing for *you*, and I held out my arms
to you and called you.   But there was
only a great silence in the room.   I have
been all wrong from the beginning, and
now it is too late.   They tell me you
are in Italy, but I will not let them send
for you, for I may die to-night, and the
thought of your coming here only to
find an empty house is intolerable to me.
But my heart aches and wearies for you.

"Perhaps if I tell you all about the
last two years it will help to bridge

them over, and make them seem less of
a gulf between us. I think death would
seem easier if I felt that to the end we
had lived our lives alongside—that there
was nothing you didn't know. When
I look back upon the time since you
went away it seems like a dream, from
which the awakening has only come
to-day. Yet there have been moments
when I have felt my heart stirring within me—once when I came across this
old photograph of us both together;
and once down by the river when
memory showed you lying unconscious
on the grass. But I would not let myself give way, partly because I felt ill
and unable to face any stress of emotion,
and partly because I regarded such feelings as weaknesses to be conquered.
For when I told you that my heart was
dead I fully believed that I was speaking
the truth, and I have believed it ever
since—till now. The strain of those

weeks before and the resolute concen‹ tration of my mind upon one idea seem to have ended in a sort of exaltation. and I was not conscious of any other motive at the time,—just as there are women who go into a convent late in life, conscious only of a religious enthusiasm, and not of the disappointments and disillusions which have gone to build it up. But when, just now, I knew that my life was over, my eyes seemed suddenly to be opened, and I saw that what I had believed to be the final victory of an idea was, after all, something very different and much more human.   There is no need for any further disguises between us, is there, Kit?   All through that time we were together I loved Ronald Gordon.   It was the one *passion* of my life, and looking back, with the clear vision of Death upon me, I know that when I closed my heart to you that night it was because I

shrank from seeing you and him together. And now all that has faded
away. Passion has died as it must
always die, and at the end of it all I am
only conscious of my love for you. The
past is all lit with it—I can't realize the
time when it was not ; it holds a torch
up to the future—for its cessation is unthinkable. So this is the end of all my
wasted years—years spent in fruitless
effort to destroy myself—that here, on
the threshold of Death, the Ego I have
tried to kill springs up into an infinitely
strengthened life, rebelling passionately
against the thought of ceasing to be,
craving only for the touch of a human
hand, now and for ever. The door
over which is written ' Loving-Kindness,' is the only door which leads into
the open. I have cramped my soul,
manacled my heart, in vain. Kit—my
beloved—I am going first ; that much is
certain. As to the rest—who knows?

But buried in my heart there is a seedlet
of hope, and looking forward I seem to
see the radiance of a coming day. I
can write no more ; the pencil seems
falling from my hand. Good-bye—good-
bye——"

Kit's head fell forward on to the open
page, and the tears, which had been
denied to her before, poured from her
eyes. But though her sense of loss
was overwhelming, the sting of it was
gone, for Susan had come back to her,
even though it were only from beyond
the grave.

THE END.

ALSO AVAILABLE FROM THOEMMES PRESS

Her Write His Name

This series makes available the forgotten works of neglected women writers whose literary contributions have been overshadowed by those of a more famous male relative. These diverse and intriguing authors can now be valued in their own right and not for the insight they give to the work of men whose name they share.

New introductions provide the social context for these writings and explain why these authors should now be allowed to shine in their own right.

Old Kensington *and* The Story of Elizabeth
Anne Isabella Thackeray
With a new introduction by Esther Schwartz-McKinzie
ISBN 1 85506 388 3 : 496pp : 1873 & 1876 editions : £17.75

Shells from the Sands of Time
Rosina Bulwer Lytton
With a new introduction by Marie Mulvey Roberts
ISBN 1 85506 386 7 : 272pp : 1876 edition : £14.75

Platonics
Ethel Arnold
With a new introduction by Phyllis Wachter
ISBN 1 85506 389 1 : 160pp : 1894 edition : £13.75

The Continental Journals 1798-1820
Dorothy Wordsworth
Edited with a new introduction by Helen Boden
ISBN 1 85506 385 9 : 472pp : New edition : £17.75

Her Life in Letters
Alice James
Edited with a new introduction by Linda Anderson
ISBN 1 85506 387 5 : 320pp : New : £15.75

Also available as a 5 volume set : ISBN 1 8556 384 0
Special set price : £70.00

For Her Own Good – A Series of Conduct Books

Cœlebs in Search of a Wife
Hannah More
With a new introduction by Mary Waldron
ISBN 1 85506 383 2 : 288pp : 1808–9 edition : £14.75

Female Replies to Swetnam the Woman-Hater
Various
With a new introduction by Charles Butler
ISBN 1 85506 379 4 : 336pp : 1615–20 edition : £15.75

A Complete Collection of Genteel and Ingenious Conversation
Jonathan Swift
With a new introduction by the Rt Hon. Michael Foot
ISBN 1 85506 380 8 : 224pp : 1755 edition : £13.75

Thoughts on the Education of Daughters
Mary Wollstonecraft
With a new introduction by Janet Todd
ISBN 1 85506 381 6 : 192pp : 1787 edition : £13.75

The Young Lady's Pocket Library, or Parental Monitor
Various
With a new introduction by Vivien Jones
ISBN 1 85506 382 4 : 352pp : 1790 edition : £15.75

Also available as a 5 volume set : ISBN 1 85506 378 6
Special Set Price: £65.00

Subversive Women

The Art of Ingeniously Tormenting
Jane Collier
With a new introduction by Judith Hawley
ISBN 1 8556 246 1 : 292pp : 1757 edition : £14.75

Appeal of One Half the Human Race, Women, Against the Pretensions of the Other Half, Men, to Retain them in Political, and thence in Civil and Domestic, Slavery
William Thompson and Anna Wheeler
With a new introduction by the Rt Hon. Michael Foot and Marie Mulvey Roberts
ISBN 1 85506 247 X : 256pp : 1825 edition : £14.75

A Blighted Life: A True Story
Rosina Bulwer Lytton
With a new introduction by Marie Mulvey Roberts
ISBN 1 85506 248 8 : 178pp : 1880 edition : £10.75

The Beth Book
Sarah Grand
With a new introduction by Sally Mitchell
ISBN 1 85506 249 6 : 560pp : 1897 edition : £18.75

The Journal of a Feminist
Elsie Clews Parsons
With a new introduction and notes by Margaret C. Jones
ISBN 1 85506 250 X : 142pp : New edition : £12.75

Also available as a 5 volume set : ISBN 1 85506 261 5
Special set price : £65.00

PHYLLIS WACHTER
is an independent scholar/educator specializing in life-writing theory and women's studies. As bibliographer for *Biography: an interdisciplinary quarterly*, she has compiled the Current Bibliography of Life-Writing for the past ten years. She is completing work on an upcoming biography about Ethel M. Arnold which was first conceived during a summer bursary awarded by Germaine Greer under the auspices of the Tulsa Center for the Study of Women's Literature.

Marie Mulvey Roberts is a Senior Lecturer in literary studies at the University of the West of England and is the author of *British Poets and Secret Societies* (1986), and *Gothic Immortals* (1990). From 1994 she has been the co-editor of a Journal: 'Women's Writing; the Elizabethan to the Victorian Period', and the General Editor for three series: *Subversive Women*, *For Her Own Good*, and *Her Write His Name*. The volumes she has co-edited include: *Sources of British Feminism* (1993), *Perspectives on the History of British Feminism* (1994), *Controversies in the History of British Feminism* (1995) and *Literature and Medicine during the Eighteenth Century* (1993). Among her single edited books are, *Out of the Night: Writings from Death Row* (1994), and editions of Rosina Bulwer Lytton's *A Blighted Life* (1994) and *Shells from the Sands of Time* (1995).

COVER ILLUSTRATION
An extract from 'After the Bath', by *Pierre-Georges Jeanniot*
Cover designed by Dan Broughton